11/26/13

Blackberry

Blossom

By Mattie Richardson

Mattie Richardson

Blackberry Blossom
Copyright © 2013
Mattie Richardson
All rights reserved.

No part of this book may be reproduced in any form, except for the inclusion of brief quotations in a review, without permission in writing from the author.

First Printing*September 2013
ISBN: 978-0-9838171-3-0

Additional copies of this and other books by Mattie Richardson are available by mail. Please see the back of the book for an order form.

Published by: MJ Richardson
www.facebook.com/Appaloosy7

Printed in the USA by
Morris Publishing®
3212 East Highway 30
Kearney, NE 68847

This book is dedicated to anyone who has helped me in any way with my musical endeavors. There are too many to list, but you know who you are and I sincerely appreciate it.

Special thanks also to Emma Marie Jameson for the picture on the cover of this book, and to Sawyer Richardson for agreeing to be in the picture with me.

Chapter 1

A young girl walked down a dirt road, alone. She was barefoot, wearing a short, dirty skirt and a faded shirt. Her light brown hair was pulled up in a ponytail, held tight by a piece of twine. Her bluish-green eyes scanned the horizon as she pulled back a piece of hair that had fallen onto her freckled face. The girl held a pair of shoes in one hand, but what really distinguished her was the violin case she carried on her back.

She hadn't seen anyone for a long time now, even though she was getting closer to a town. She needed to get to the town before nightfall if she wanted some supper. She continued down the road at a good pace, humming to herself softly. Rows of dried-out corn stood on either side of her and she was just beginning to see the buildings of the city in the distance. Her stomach growled loudly.

The girl turned her head when she heard what sounded like a creaking wagon driving up behind her. She saw an old wagon pulled by a pair of skinny horses making their way down the road. She didn't take much notice. There were a lot of travelers these days, and not a lot of people bothered to give the less fortunate rides anymore.

She was surprised when the wagon stopped beside her and looked up to see an old fellow peering down at her.

"Where're you going?" He asked gruffly.

She hesitated in answering for a second, not sure if it was alright to go with this man. She decided that he looked kind enough, and she was sure that she could get away and outrun him if she had to.

"Milesville," she answered.

"I'm heading that way, too, if you want a ride."

The girl looked tired, like she had been walking all day, and the man knew she couldn't be much more than sixteen years old, so he was happy to give her a ride. He stretched out his hand to help her up onto the wagon seat. She accepted it and climbed up beside him gratefully. He snapped the long leather reins and the wagon jolted ahead.

"So what'd be your name?" he asked her.

"Molly," she told him carefully, "Molly Turner."

Of course, her last name wasn't really "Turner;" her last name was almost always different, depending on who she was talking to.

"And what confounded thing have you got strapped onto your back?" He asked curiously.

She looked at his long white beard and then into his dark eyes, evaluating him. "I've got a fiddle."

"Can you play it?"

They heard a blast from a car horn behind them and the man barely had time to move the wagon aside before the car flew by them, spooking the horses into a fast trot. He pulled them down to a walk again and cursed the man and his car.

"Of course I can play it," Molly interrupted his profanities.

He sighed and gazed ahead into the road. "I'd like to hear you."

"I hope to play at a restaurant or tavern tonight for my supper. If I'm able to, I'd be glad to have you watch my performance," she said.

They were both silent, and the wagon continued to creak down the road, slowly away from the sunset and toward the town.

Molly thanked the man then climbed down from the wagon and started walking down the street to look for places to play. She had been traveling for almost a year now, playing in bars and taverns, for dances and weddings, special occasions and sometimes even for the people in the collection of cardboard and tin shacks called "Hoovervilles". So far she had been lucky enough to keep from starving, but as times got harder and people became even tighter with their money and food, even a bite to eat could sometimes be hard to come by.

She walked into a small café and asked to speak with the manager. As she waited for him the smell of warm food cooking in the kitchen wafted to her nostrils, and she tried not to drool. The person in charge of the place came to her only a few minutes later. "I was wondering if you'd like to have a fiddle player entertain your dinning guests tonight?" Molly asked with a smile.

She looked around and saw a couple of guests eating, but the place was far from full. The forks and spoons clattered loudly in the near-vacant room. How she envied people who could not only afford food, but could afford to have people cook their food and serve it to them!

The manager frowned. "We don't have money to pay you," he told her.

"That's alright, all I ask is a bite to eat and a place to sleep."

He still looked skeptical.

But before he could answer she pulled the case off her back and put it onto the arms of a chair. She took out the bow and rosined it carefully with her small, precious chuck of rosin, then pulled out the violin and tucked it under her chin.

She played "Blackberry Blossom" for him, keeping her eyes on his face. When she had finished he shook his head.

"You don't like fiddle music? Well I can play slow, sweet violin solos too." She pulled the bow slowly across the strings and let out a melodious song.

He interrupted her. "I'm sorry but we just can't have you tonight. Now get out or I'll have a waiter throw you out!"

She sighed disappointedly while she put the old violin back into its case. Tugging the strap to pull her violin case behind her back, she went out the doors and looked for another place. She would try a small tavern she had seen on the other side of town. Molly usually tried to avoid bars, she remembered her mother telling her of all the problems alcohol had given their family. But taverns were usually much fuller, and while people didn't have money to spend on a fancy dinner for two, most of them always had a few cents to spare for some booze or whiskey.

Molly shook her head. She didn't want to think about her family. She walked into the bar, asking the same question of the owner there. He looked a little doubtful though, as well.

"My act lasts about an hour," she started, "I usually take a short intermission, and while I do that I sure can don an apron and bring out orders." She told him.

"Well, I'll make you a deal," he said. "Play for them and you can have supper. If they like it, I'll let you keep any tips you get and you can have a room for the night. But if they don't like it I won't hesitate to let them throw you out."

She was pleased. Molly knew that good, decent men and women always loved her act. "Yes!" she said, "you have a deal!"

"Then go upstairs. Charlotte will see that you get a warm bath. Make sure to be down here at eight."

"Yes sir!" She said and turned to go upstairs.

The tavern owner and his family lived above the tavern. Molly found their home quite comfortable and was pleased when she received a real bath, with warm water and soap. After shaking the dirt out of them and rubbing out wrinkles, she put her same clothes back on, then tied up the laces to her only pair of shoes.

A lot of people would probably grumble about the life Molly faced every day. She had no home, no family, no steady income and very few possessions. But Molly didn't care, she had spent most of her life as a vagrant and so she knew that there were people better off than she, and there were people who had it much, much worse. She had seen some of them.

She combed out her hair with the little metal comb she kept in the small compartment hidden away in her violin case, then parted it and braided it into two long braids. She took a good look at herself before she went downstairs. Molly was glad that she had landed this gig. Opportunities were getting harder to find here in the Midwest; she told herself that if they got too far and in between she just might have to hop a train heading east.

She grabbed her fiddle and headed downstairs. The room was smoky and smelled bad but there were quite a few guests seated around the tables. Talk went on all around her.

When Molly had first started playing "professionally", she found it hard to speak up and her voice wavered. Her fingers shook as she slid them up and down the neck of her old fiddle, and she scratched some of her tunes. But now she was confident.

American people nowdays may have liked the sounds of the evolving Jazz music or Swing, but Molly knew her music was just as danceable with a good beat. The bluegrass music she played was slowly fading away as more popular, modern music took over, but Molly wasn't going to let her music die without a fight.

She climbed up on a small homemade stage up front, then ripped out in a song called "Boil the Cabbage". It was a favorite, and as her fingers moved around her violin she grinned at the crowd. The talk began to cease, and that was good. Sometimes there were arrogant people in a crowd that refused to even pay attention. She added a few pitzacattos and trick fiddling. She jumped off the stage and made her way through the tables, winking at a few of the younger lads and making her skirt swirl around her. Molly had often practiced dancing alone with her fiddle on the road, now she perfected it.

Before she knew it the song was over and she was back on the stage. "Hey now how do you think that new president is doing in the White House?" She asked the crowd loudly.

"He's gotta be better than Hoover, huh?!?"

A loud boo came from the crowd.

"Well at least I hope so!"

She told a few jokes to the crowd, most of them concerning the hard times no one could avoid. The crowd laughed animatedly, howling sometimes, and Molly had a hard time discerning whether it was from their drinks or if she was really that funny.

She played a few slow waltzes, and played a short tune, "Rubber Dolly." She put her fiddle by her side and sung the words to the crowd:

My momma told me,

If I be a goodie,

That she would buy me,

A rubber dolly,

So don't you tell her,

I've got a feller,

Or she won't buy me,

A rubber dolly!

The crowd applauded hysterically, and ordered more drinks. Molly thought it would be a good time to crawl off the stage and grab an apron for her intermission. She excused herself and put her fiddle in the case behind the counter where she was sure no one could steal it.

She brought the food from the kitchen and served people right and left. Molly couldn't be more happy. Although the place she decided to play in was rather rough, the people certainly enjoyed the music and she even got a few tips.

After the atmosphere calmed down a little she got back up onto the stage. She played some lively hoedowns and a song she had made up herself. Then her eyes sparkled as she jumped into the air for one of her favorites, "Devil's Dream". Her arm got to moving so fast it felt like it was going to break, and her braids swung vigorously around her face, but it was worth it! This is what she loved to do. She switched strings and went faster and faster. The men were tapping their feet to the beat, which was getting harder as she went faster. Her palms grew sweaty and finally the song got to be too fast for her and she tripped on a note. The crowd laughed, and Molly took a bow.

She glanced up at the big old clock on the other side of the room. Ten o'clock already! How did it get to be so late? She concluded her act and made her way to the front of the tavern, her arms shaking exhaustedly. She sat up on one of the stools where the bar owner's daughter served her a warm plate of food. Molly was almost too tired to eat it but she slowly forked the nourishing food into her mouth.

She didn't notice a figure move up beside her. A young man leaned on the counter and looked at her.

"Do you really got a feller, miss?" He asked.

Molly looked up from her food at the man. His long blond hair fell into his face, and he was a fairly handsome fellow, but Molly didn't like the way his eyes were bloodshot red.

Of course she didn't have a feller, and she didn't intend to get one. "No." She answered honestly.

"Well, good 'cause I didn't feel like beatin' one up for you."

"I don't have a man and I have no plans for getting one."

"Well, how old are ya anyway?" he asked.

"I'm eighteen," she answered. Even though Molly had different last names, she always had the same age. She couldn't let anyone know that she was only sixteen.

"I think that's kinda young to be out on the road," he warned. Molly stared at him. She was tired and hungry and didn't feel like talking, especially to a half-drunk man who just wanted to bother her. She glanced at the bar owner, her eyes pleading for help. The friendly man nodded slightly.

"Curse you, Jesse, leave the girl alone!" He walked towards the man.

"Aw, I only wanna have a little fun," Jesse whined, but didn't move. The bar owner glared at him. He stood right where he was beside Molly. They stayed that way for awhile, staring silently. It seemed as if all the eyes in the room were on them.

Molly's fingers ran over the small pocketknife she always kept with her, but her hand pulled out of her pocket and she calmly took a sip of her ginger ale, wiped her chin and then stood up. "You are quite the gentleman," she told the man sarcastically, and then picked up her foot and smashed it into his kneecap.

"Owww!' he screeched. "Why I ougta . . ." He reached for her but Molly dashed behind the counter.

Molly's foot throbbed through her thin-soled shoes, but she only stared defiantly at the man. He glared at her with bloodshot eyes.

"Out!" The bartender yelled, "Get out of here now!"

The man finally left, but not before giving Molly another awful glare. Molly sat back down and continued to eat her food, only a little shaken by the experience.

"Well, I see that you are a little too used to defending yourself," the bar owner told her when things settled down. "How long have you been by yourself?"

"I'm not by myself, my parents live out of town and I just come over here to make a little money and to get out of the house. I don't really like farming, or my parents," she said nervously.

He knew that she was lying. But he also knew that she would bring in more people to his establishment if she performed again, so he didn't push it. "Well," he said, "if it's alright with your parents, you could stay another night if you want to perform. The audience loved your act."

The two looked at each other, both of them trying to decipher what the other was thinking. "Okay," she said finally. "My parents said I could stay as long as I could find work."

She pushed her plate away and stood up off the stool. "I'd better turn in then," she said, then turned to go upstairs. She barely had time to crawl underneath the covers of a small guest bed before she was fast asleep.

The next night there were even more people than the first. The bar owner had asked her to stay one more night, but Molly had refused, saying that she wanted to keep her act fresh.

The morning she planned to leave she rose early. Only the bar owner's wife was up, everyone else was sound asleep. Sunlight streamed over her and her shadow hovered around the room as she opened her fiddle case and pulled out its contents, looking them over carefully. Of course there was her fiddle, the old fiddle that had been her grandfather's. He was the one who had shown her how to play it, and he had taught her well. By now she was better than a lot of adults that knew how to play.

She opened the small compartment inside the case. Inside there was rosin, she had always used the stuff very sparingly as a new box could cost as much as fifteen cents. Her metal comb was still safely inside, as well as her bar of soap she kept in case she had nowhere to stay, and a pair of pants she usually wore for traveling. She switched her skirt for the pants and laid the skirt on the table. She then pulled a little pouch out from the case. This is what she put her money in. Molly emptied it and carefully counted out the change. She had $1.35. Rarely did she spend the money, she always kept most of it in case she became ill or had to go back home.

 Home. Underneath all of her other things was a small folded photograph. She opened it up to see her mother and her father, then Molly herself and her two brothers in black and white. The boys wore overalls and had dirty faces that were frowning into the camera. Their shack was not far behind them and a tall windmill rose up in the background. Her father frowned as well, and he held a horse by the bridle. Her mother made an attempt to smile, but it didn't turn out quite right. Molly glared expressionless, her hair fell into her eyes and over her freckles, and she wore a faded dress.

A traveling photographer had offered to take a picture of them on their farm, her momma had said yes and her dad had, too, until he had to pay the photographer for it. He was mad then.
She took the photograph when she had run away from home. It was the only one that her family had, but she figured that she would need it more than they did. She loved her family but she couldn't take it anymore. She had to get away.
Molly forced the memory from her mind and folded up the photograph and set it carefully back into the case. She arranged the other things and stuffed the skirt on top. She shut the case quickly and latched it. The sun was coming up over the horizon very quickly. She silently crept down the stairs and went out the door, latching it quietly before she set off on the road again.

She kept on traveling. Molly didn't know exactly where she was, but she figured that she was somewhere in the eastern part of Indiana. She needed to keep moving east. East meant more people. And more people—hopefully-- meant more food and money.
  Molly traveled along a river and soon began to see another city on the horizon. She moved toward it confidently; she was used to traveling and her tough bare feet were ready for a thousand miles more. The closer she got to the city the more trash she saw around and in the river. Molly stopped before she thought it got too bad.
  She peered into the water and took a good look at herself. Molly set her case down on a dry patch of grass and opened it up to pull out her little metal comb. She combed out her fuzzy braids back into a pony tail. She knelt on the bank and looked into the water.
  Her green eyes gazed back at her and she smiled. Her bony fingers ran through her hair to straighten it out. She just couldn't see what any man could see in her. She was just a scrawny traveling musician (and even that was a nice way to put it) who still had freckles and still acted

a bit boyish at times. Yes, she was alone but she was well able to take care of herself. She didn't need anybody.

Molly heard something behind her, and turned to see a woman with a small basket making her way to the river. She was singing an old tune and other voices joined her as she walked toward the riverbank. Molly considered jumping in and swimming to the other side, but the women looked quite harmless so she stayed where she was in the grass and listened to them singing.

About six women finally came to the bank and pulled out dirty laundry from the baskets and buckets that they carried. They scrubbed the clothes vigorously on the rocks near the riverbank, some of them had soap while others had to do without. None of them paid much attention to Molly.

The song was soon over after they began to wash their clothing. They chatted quietly with one other and washed small feed sack dresses and trousers carefully, trying not to have them ripped.

"That was a beautiful song you sang," Molly told one of the older women when they had finished as she came closer to them. The woman wrung out a shirt and hung it on a tree branch to dry.

"The song is called 'Angel Band'," she replied, "Or at least that's what we always called it."

Molly looked at the woman's silvery hair and kind brown eyes, then sat on the ground next to her and helped the woman wring out her husband's pair of trousers. "I am a musician," she said to the woman, "and I travel around trying to discover as many songs as I can. Could you please sing that one for me again?"

The woman steadily sang the tune while she finished her washing.

My latest sun is sinking fast, my race is nearly run
My strongest trials now are past, my triumph is begun
O come, Angel Band, come and around me stand
O bear me away on your snowy wings to my immortal home!

The woman's voice was amazing as she slowly let out the rest of the song. Molly sat in the grass beside her, patiently listening to the song and absorbing the lyrics. When the woman was finished, Molly was sure to thank and praise her for it.

"Would you sing it one more time?" she asked. "Just to make sure I've got all the words right."

The woman started again, and Molly joined in singing the harmony. Her voice searched a little for just the right notes, but all in all she sang the tune beautifully.

Together the pair walked back from the river, Molly helping to carry some of the wet clothing while they both sang. Molly didn't know where she was following the woman to, but as long as the song went on, she trailed behind her.

The two followed closely behind the group of women until they had caught up to them. The group continued down the slope toward the city. But before they got to the city, they came to a large shantytown full of people situated on the outskirts of the little city. Some children ran out to meet them, others played nearby and bathed in the dirty river.

Molly noticed that the majority of the people in the town were African-American, although there were a good piece of them who were white. They all wore dirty clothes that hung loosely on their thin frames, some of them were lucky enough to have worn shoes. A lot of them eyed Molly and her violin suspiciously, she pulled the case closer to her back and gripped the strap tightly.

The houses in this "city" were made of scrap tin and sometimes even cardboard. Some of the younger single men slept in tents that were full of holes. In what was nearly the middle of the town lay a huge bonfire with a lot of people warming themselves next to it.

"Who's that?"

A demanding voice broke into Molly's evaluation of the Hooverville. She looked over to see a dark face scowling at her. It belonged to a tall dark man who sat next to the fire, his jaw was hard-set and he had an old derby hat on his head. He had bushy eyebrows that curved down into his scowl, but his eyes, Molly thought, still had a hint of kindness in them. He had an air about him that he was in charge.

The old woman looked at him with glazed eyes. "She's a musician, Silas, come to make our days just a little bit more merry," she told him. The man called Silas still looked skeptically at her. He was in charge of this shantytown, and he didn't like strangers just busting in and making themselves right at home. Especially ones that looked fairly fortunate and had a northern accent.

Before Silas could say anything else, Molly answered for herself. "My name is Molly Green, performer and fine musician, and in exchange for some supper and a place to stay for the night, I would be glad to play a few tunes for you."

The man's eyes softened and he reconsidered. *A runaway*, he thought silently.

"Sure ya can," he answered audibly, "we ain't had any music around here for quite some time now, we'd be pleased to have ya. We ain't got the best pickin's as far as food goes, but it'll be good for ya and will stick to them bones."

Stout sticks were arranged so that a woman was able to hang a pot full of water over the fire and it began to boil. She pulled out a wooden spoon and began to stir the water. And then came the people. Each person brought a little bit of what he had, a little radish, a few green beans, and maybe even a piece of meat cut into tiny pieces. They added it to the pot along with some salt and pepper and the woman kept stirring. Molly watched quietly from the sidelines with interest.

Pulling out her violin carefully, Molly looked over the people's sad expressions.

This is what she was here for.

She rosined up her bow and tucked the violin under her chin. She chopped out a verse on her fiddle, immediately grabbing people's attention, then sang it out,

> *Went up on the mountain top*
> *Just to give my horn a blow,*
> *Thought I heard my true love say*
> *"Yonder comes my beau!"*

She put the violin back in its place and the crowd that had gathered sang the chorus.

*Bile them cabbage down, down, turn them hoecakes round.
The only song that I can sing is bile dem cabbage down!*

With a smile on her face she continued on down every verse she knew.

*Once I had an old gray mule,
His name was Simon Slick,
He'd roll his eyes and back his ears,
And how that mule would kick!*

The people loved it! All the way to verse seven they followed Molly's violin. The farther she got the crazier she became, kicking up her heels and dancing with her fiddle. When it was over the crowd of people cheered her on for another song, but Silas rang out in his deep voice, "DINNER'S READY!" and all grabbed a tin plate or dish to get served.

The children were first, followed by the women and then the men. Molly was handed a plate and she made her way into the line with the others. The sun was hanging low in the sky and Molly looked dreamily into the sunset, then shifted her eyes over to the small city that rose up in the near distance.

She knew that she didn't know everything, but Molly knew that she loved her life. She was sure that she could do this every day. Why, she did do it every day! The wind blew her skirt gently against her thin legs, the coolness of spring still on them. The air smelled of smoke. Chatter went on all around her, and occasionally to her, but she was still deep in thought.

"Here you go, missy," Some of the steaming food was ladled onto her plate. The people found places all around to sit and enjoy their meal, some by the fire, some leaning their backs on trees, and others on turned over wooden tubs or even chairs. Molly sat next to the fire and took a look at her food. It was somewhat like a runny soup, with green beans and cabbage and some kind of meat. She wasn't sure which kind of meat was in it, but she didn't care. Food was food. She gobbled it down.

"I didn't know that there was female players of the violin that were just as darn good as the men," Silas was saying.

Molly brought her head up and frowned.

He caught a glimpse of her scowling face and laughed. "But she rocked this boat!" he benevolently complimented her. "That girl is one of the best. I can't believe that I haven't ever heard of her before." Some of the people applauded in agreement.

The conversation turned to another subject and Molly continued to eat her meal, her eyes drifting dozily as she spooned the stuff into her mouth. Her eyes searched all the faces, she felt like she should talk to someone, but still she sat alone. Molly was an entertainer. A performer. Someone that people admired and looked up to. But no one talked to her, and so she talked to no one, but made her way to the shack where she was given a cot to sleep in.

It was dark now, and so she stretched herself out in the small cot and yawned, then turned over and fell asleep.

Light streamed in through the cracks in the small shanty the next morning, pouring over Molly's face and awakening her from her slumber. She stretched and reached for her violin. Her heart nearly stopped. Where was her violin?

She frantically swung around and fell hard on the floor of the shanty. She stood on her knees and spat out the dirt that had gotten into her mouth and continued looking.

"Oh, sweetheart, don't worry yourself so!" Molly looked up to see a black woman chiding her for her frenzied search.

"You leaned it up against the wall last night but I knew it wouldn't be safe with all these tramps and desperate people wandering around the city at night, so it's hidden behind the wall." The woman said, pointing.

Molly looked at her, surprised and speechless. "Well, go along, go git it out!" The woman told her, and then she stepped back outside.

Molly regained her composure and found the old violin case behind the wall, just as the woman had told her. Molly exhaled in relief. She combed back her hair, then stuffed her thin metal comb into her pocket and then went out the door. How could she have slept so late? It must have been at least seven.

Most of the men were out of the town and in the city, either looking for a job or for handouts. Both were scarce, and Molly knew that many of the men would return empty handed. The woman and children took care of things around the Hooverville, finding wild fruits and vegetables to eat and doing the household chores.

Down the little alley she went, Molly was looking for the woman so she could properly thank her for letting her sleep in her house. She was hard to find, with so many unfamiliar faces and names, but soon enough Molly did find her and thank her, asking that she also would thank Silas for her. Molly needed to be on her way.

She continued on at a lazy pace down the road, getting closer to the city. She still was next to the river, the long river she had followed for the last thirty or forty miles. Cars passed frequently down the road, and she was sure to stay on the side away from their speeding wheels and annoying horns. The cool spring breeze blew through her hair and birds sang quietly. Molly relished the warm sunshine that bathed her face in its glorious rays.

"You darn thief, that's my nickel!"

Molly wasn't far from the shantytown when she heard voices and some scuffing not far away from her. Her attention was diverted for just a minute but she decided to ignore it and continue on.

"You tall Yank, you're just a fool who's got himself puffed up over--"

Whack!

Molly heard someone land a punch, and then she couldn't resist going over to see what was happening. She followed the noises until she saw two boys fighting. Over what, she wasn't exactly sure. She kneeled down in the bushes to watch.

One of the boys was a short, slightly pudgy kid with dark hair covered by a newsboy hat. He wore overall suspenders and a dirty shirt, and one of his eyes was getting dark and puffy. The other boy was at least a head taller, but he was pretty lanky. His face was covered with freckles and he had the strangest rust-colored hair Molly had ever seen that hung in his face over his eyes. He wore pants that hung above his ankles, much too short for him, and his fists were held up, his face twisted into an angry scowl. But somehow his eyes were smiling, and the corners of his mouth threatened it, like he was just putting on his game face for the fight. They were almost men, but the way they were fighting told Molly that they were still to be called boys. They looked about as old as Molly.

Whack! Another punch was thrown. *I've got to do something,* Molly thought to herself, *or they both are going to kill each other.*

She emerged from the bushes. The fighting continued; between punches the two swearing and cussing at each other. "Hey," she said meekly in an attempt to get their attention. Nothing happened.

"Hey!" She shouted louder. The two stopped and looked at her. "That's no way to behave! You're going to hurt each other if you keep that up." They continued to look at her for a moment, then kept on with their fighting.

Molly was angry. Why wouldn't they listen to her, or at least even acknowledge her presence? She was simmering, and was just about to give up and leave, but she could sense herself losing her temper and so she stayed. Molly walked up right between the two boys fighting, right into the middle of the dust, the yelling and the striking and frowned. They stopped, and before they knew what she was doing, she reached up and boxed one of the guys' ears, then the other.

"Now shoo, you two asses, and go do something useful with your lives."

The shorter boy rubbed his ears for a second, then realized that now was the time to get out of the fight if he wanted to, and turned and started running back to the shantytown. The taller boy considered chasing after him, but his eyes were fixed on the girl.

"You're the girl who played violin last night in that Hooverville, aren't you?" He asked, rubbing his ears.

Molly started to walk away. The boy followed. "Molly—right?"

"Yes," she answered.

"Where are you headed to?" He asked.

"I don't know," Molly answered, "I think I'm going east. That's all I know. I'm sort of a wanderer."

"I can tell," he laughed. Molly ignored him.

"What is your name, then?" Molly asked him.

"My name?" he said, "I'm Pepper."

"Pepper?" she asked. "What kind of name is that?"

"I don't know," he said, "I think people mainly call me that because of these kid freckles I have, even though I'm seventeen years old."

"Well, I still have freckles over my nose, and I'm--" She stopped before she disclosed her age to him. "Don't you have a family or something? You should be working, or at least looking for work like everyone else."

She didn't let him answer. "You need to get out of here now. I travel alone, and I have important business to see to. I don't need some kid bothering me to kingdom come. Now shoo, I said!"

He looked at her for a second longer, then left. Molly was surprised at herself. She sure seemed to be bossy a lot of the time. And why did she keep calling him kid? He was at least four inches taller than she, and older, too apparently. There was something strange about him, she thought, but she threw the thought from her mind because she was nearing the outskirts of the city.

Chapter 2

Molly didn't get to the cities very often. Most of her traveling was through farmland and small towns, rarely did she get to pass through a large city. But she was a farm girl at heart, and she was aware of the danger that lurked everywhere in such a big place. The place smelled of smoke and garbage, kind of like the shantytown but ten times worse. Dirty jobless men sat on street corners, begging or trying to make some kind of a living selling fruits or trinkets.

Her eyes were downcast when she passed these men. Life was hard out on the farm, but it could be much harder here in the city. She remembered hearing that unemployment had reached rates of almost thirty percent in some places. Molly couldn't imagine what it would be like to live in a place where almost one out of every three people didn't have a job, or means to provide for themselves or their families.

Tall gray buildings rose up on either side of her as Molly made her way down the street. She was trying to decide. Molly couldn't decide if she should try to find someplace to play here in the city, or should she just make her way through as quickly as possible, knowing that being an unknown person in the city was especially dangerous at night.

She passed a theater, with a line of people waiting for the afternoon's movie. They laughed and talked as they waited to pay for their tickets, happily anticipating the film. Molly stood behind them for a moment, contemplating if she had a nickel to spare for such a luxury. Well, she knew that she did have a nickel to spare, but how could she spend it on something so meaningless; so fun?

No, the nickel could be spent on much better things, she thought. She turned away from the building and continued on through the crowds of people, turning into a dark alley against her better judgment. It was quieter down that way, and Molly thought that maybe it would serve as a shortcut to getting out of this city.

Suddenly two tall men swept up behind her. They each grabbed one of her arms, and rushed with her into another alley. "Hey!!" she shouted, trying only to catch anyone's attention so that they could come to her rescue. "Let me go you ruffians!" She struggled but it was no use. The two were much stronger than she, and held her feet a couple inches off the ground. They quickly climbed down some stairs and entered into a dark building.

The men threw her on her feet when they were inside. Molly blinked, trying to see in the dim light of the apartment.

"We've got something," one of the men said.

A big man raised himself out of a chair and looked over to Molly. "Well, what do we have here?" he said. Molly glared at the man. What did he want with her? He smoked a cigar and the smell made Molly want to throw up. She coughed. "What is that you have on your back? Some sort of musical instrument?"

"It's a fiddle," she replied angrily.

"Well, are your parents living somewhere near to here?" He asked her.

"Well, um," she started.

"Do you know that it is against the law to be wandering aimlessly around the city? I could have you arrested for vagrancy."

"I not wandering around aimlessly," she shouted angrily, "I'm a musician, and I'm on my way through this city."

"Well, a musician would be handy on our way to California," he said. "We need a girl to do cooking and other chores, as my two chums here aren't so keen on the work. It would keep you out of getting arrested, you would have some food in your belly and place to stay. And we would treat you nice," he said with a disturbing grin.

"California?" Molly said with awe. "I'm heading in completely the opposite direction!" She ran at the door, but was caught roughly by one of the men. She kicked, screamed and punched with all her might.

"She's no good!" The man said, "Lock her in the closet and we'll see what we can do with her tomorrow." The man pried the violin case off her back and flung it against the wall. He threw Molly in the closet and locked the door.

Molly sat on a pile of dusty, stinky clothes. She was quiet for a moment in the still darkness, but then began pounding on the door. "Let me out!" she screamed and cursed at him, "Let me out!"

She soon tired and plopped down onto the clothes, listening to the men's conversation. They seemed to be talking of money, and they were going through the items in her violin case. Silent tears streamed down her face. *Oh please, don't let them take my violin!* she quietly begged. Molly peeked through a small keyhole in the door. They quickly found her dollar and thirty-five cents, and stuffed that into their pockets. As for the violin rosin and the fiddle itself, they threw back in the case.

"We can sell it to Jerry at the pawn shop tomorrow. That is, if you do want to turn in the girl," one of the men said.

"Na. We'll let her go. It's been profitable enough taking her stuff. It was quite a bit of fun, scaring her like that, and we should make plenty on the fiddle. But for now, we've got to go." The man grabbed a bottle of booze, and headed out the door with the others following him.

Molly really let the tears flow. She had never been in such a pickle before. Here she was, locked in a closet with her poor violin destined to be pawned. What could she do? It was so bad that she almost . . . well, wanted her ma and pa. But she was too old for that now. She cleared her head and thought. She had to get out.

She kicked the door as hard as she was able, but nothing happened and the door stood where it was. Molly sat down to think. What could she do? She dug around the pile of things she was sitting on, searching through the darkness for something that she could use. Once again she peered through the keyhole.

It was a simple lock, she could tell. All she would need to do is find something to sort of pry the lock the other way. What could she use? Molly was glad that the men had been too stupid to bind her up as she dug through the things in the closet.

But wait! Hadn't it been obvious? Her hands immediately went to her pocket on the side of her skirt. Inside was her comb, the one she had left inside that very morning! How glad Molly was that for once she had been too lazy to put it back inside of her case. She smiled inside the dark closet and began to twist the thin metal around to a shape that she could use to unlock the door.

Again and again Molly tried, and as she did, she thought about her day. She was sorry that she hadn't spent the stupid nickel on the movie now, she wouldn't have been in this predicament if she would have. Her fingers blistered with the many hurried attempts to twist the little comb into the perfect shape to open the simple lock. But she had to hurry. She didn't know when the men would be back! She stuffed it into the keyhole one last time and twisted it. *Click!* It worked! She quietly pushed the door open and blinked in the light. Her eyes instantly fell to her fiddle. She ran over to it and gently rearranged the items and shut the case. Molly threw it over her back and quickly, but quietly, made her way outside.

Once outside, she fairly flew down the city streets, her thin-soled shoes slapping noisily on the pavement. Now she knew that she wasn't going to stay in the city, she was getting out of there as soon as she could. The sun was beginning to set in the west, and she still had a mile or two left to go to get to the outskirts on the other side.

Molly ran through the smog and toward the end of the city. She ignored everyone on either side of the street until she had gotten safely to the edge of the terrible place. Her legs trembled as she walked, but she forced herself to keep going far into the night.

Around midnight, she came to a small farm. She didn't even bother asking, she opened the door to the barn and walked inside. The smell of fresh hay was welcoming. There were only a few horses and a cow inside, so she made herself at home in a large pile of freshly-cut prairie hay and was soon fast asleep.

Chapter 3

"What are ya doin' in my barn!" Molly's eyes shot open at the accusation suddenly being made at her. A tall, older man with thin gray hair and spectacles was staring right at her, with a pitchfork in his hands. Molly barely had time to jump before he was poking it at her sides, chasing her out of the barn as fast as he could go.

Molly flew out the door and continued running down the road.

"And stay out you rotten tramp!" He yelled. Molly paid no attention, but ran down the road and out of sight until her sides ached. How could she have done that? She should have asked first, but at the very least she could have woke up before the farmer had and she would have saved herself being stabbed at.

Tramp.

That's what he called her. And that is what she was. It just seemed to be a sort of revelation to her now. Molly had only been out on the road for a few months, but she had never encountered so much trouble in so little time. She was homeless, hungry and didn't have a penny to her name.

Molly hung her head and continued down the road.

Molly traveled on uneventfully for the next couple days. She played at a few places, keeping her belly full enough and making about twenty cents in the process. The road she traveled had flared out and had not gone in the right direction for her so she began to travel through the woods on a small worn trail.

She was traveling quietly, with the thoughts of the past week still on her mind. The warm sun of June splashed down on her back and kept her warm. Molly enjoyed the change of scenery, the green cottonwood trees and aspens were especially beautiful and smelled delicious compared to the city smog. In the beautiful surroundings her mind wandered. She had to keep moving, she needed more people with fresh ears for fiddle music. Molly continued to ponder, until she suddenly heard a strange noise near the trees. She gasped when she thought that she saw a figure move between two trees.

Molly stopped tersely and looked around, but the noise had stopped. She cautiously began moving again, keeping an eye out for anything strange. She walked quietly along the trail until

CRASH! Tree branches whipped around and a figure fell from the tree ahead of her, and a jumble of arms and legs fell into a pile right ahead of her. She kept from screaming, but her eyes widened and she prepared to run. But wait. That orange hair was familiar.

Pepper!

"What on earth are you doing here?" Molly asked.

Pepper pulled a twig from his hair, and straightened himself out. Ignoring her question, he said, "I've heard your fiddle music and I think it's great, but you know, I think you're missing one thing."

"And what would that be?" Molly asked him.

"A guitar backup," he said, "would make people come from miles around just to hear the pair play in any establishment."

"Hmm." Molly said, "I wonder where I could find one of those." She then made her way around him and continued on her way down the trail.

He ran up in front of her and forced her to stop. "Well, you're looking at one."

"Okay then, where's the guitar?"

"Well," he stammered and turned a little red, "I was thinking that maybe you could help me with that one. I thinking that a good one would cost about a dollar, and I've got thirty cents."

She sighed. "Well, you're out of luck, I've been cleaned out of nearly every penny I have and now all I've got is two dimes. Altogether we still need fifty more cents. And I'm still not charmed with your proposition anyway, but I am with the fact that you followed me all the way over here."

He grinned cockily. "I've got no home, and you haven't either, so I thought maybe it'd be good if we stuck together. Two together is stronger than one. And it would help you from getting into scrapes like the one you got into that day in the city with those drunks."

So he knew about what happened to her in the city. She suddenly shrunk back, embarrassed. Molly was about to ask him what business he had anyway, following her like that, but she didn't feel like talking about it anymore and so just said, "Alright. You can come along, if you earn your keep and such. And try not to bother me too much."

Pepper smiled. "You bet I will!"

"Besides," she said, "I do know a song called 'Red Haired Boy'"

And so Molly set off once again down the narrow trail, with the boy Pepper following close behind.

The two traveled through the woods silently for a couple hours, until Pepper pulled out a pack of cigarettes. He lit a match and put it up to the cigarette between his teeth. Molly turned and looked at him disgustedly.

"What?" he asked. "You want one?" He blew out a stream of smoke.

"No." She said. "I don't believe I do." Molly paused for a moment, then asked, "Hey, how much do you have left in that pack?"

"About four or five, but they oughta last me until we get to the next city."

"A boy your age shouldn't be smoking already. I think that we should see if we can sell them to anyone or if they'll trade."

"Awww," Pepper started.

"You don't have to worry about that. I'm not forcing you to stay with me. You could go back to your kin and smoke all you want."

"I don't have any kin," Pepper stated, "They all died off of the fever, only a couple months ago. I tried living in the shantytown, and I tried finding a job in the city, but it just didn't work. I was going ta hop a train heading to California but I missed it. And then you came along. I think I could make it as a traveling musician," he said, acting just a bit cocky.

Molly was silent for a moment, until Pepper inquired, "Well what happened to your ma and pa?"

"I flew."

"Where did ya leave from?" Pepper asked.

"Nebraska."

Molly didn't want to talk about it.

Pepper whistled. "Wow, all the way from Nebraska and you're still making out alright? You must be doing pretty good out here all by yourself. For a girl, anyway."

Molly ignored him.

"Well, are you just roaming around or do you plan on settlin' down somewhere?" He asked, starting the conversation again.

"I'm not sure," Molly answered, glad for the opportunity to change the subject. "I'm making out pretty good around here but I think I could do better if I went to New York. Hopefully I could get a permanent gig or maybe even get on with a band or something like that."

"We could be on the radio!" Pepper announced, "we could tell jokes and stuff in addition to playing music. Who knows?"

Who said anything about we? Molly thought. But she doubted it, anyway. But she liked the way Pepper thought about it. Big ideas, he had. She almost chuckled. "Well, we'll see about that."

"We'll have a long time to talk about it, anyway, see's how we're only in eastern Illinois." Pepper pointed out.

They were getting close to another small town now. Buildings rose up on the horizon, and the smell of food frying in the distance set Molly's mouth to watering. She closed her eyes and thought for a moment. Her feet ached, and she was ready for a bit of a rest.

"It's not proper for a girl and boy our age to be traveling together, you know," Molly told him.

Pepper grinned. "It's not proper for you to be traveling alone either, is it?" He asked. "And it's not proper for me to be smoking cigarettes or swearing or anything like that, but I do it anyway. A lot of things aren't proper but we do 'em."

Molly thought for a second but chose to ignore his commentary. "This town looks like a pleasant place. I don't think that we'll have much trouble, and if we can find a place to stay we'll stay for a couple days. In that time you could make yourself useful and find a little work. A job here and there, a nickel there and a quarter here, and if I can get a good amount of tips we'll have enough to buy a secondhand guitar in no time."

Pepper smiled and raised his eyebrows. "And just how far are you willing to go to get good tips?"

Molly couldn't help herself that time, she slapped him hard.

"Ow," he whined. "I was just joshin'."

"Well I am at least that proper," she said sullenly.

The town was a sorry sight, it hadn't been missed by the depression. The people seemed resourceful, however, as many town houses had gardens in the front and chicken coops tucked away in the back yard.

"I wonder where we can get a good bite to eat?" Molly asked aloud. "I don't know if there are any good restaurants or taverns around here."

They didn't have to search for long before they found one. They inquired inside, but were turned away. Molly sagged her shoulders and looked down to the ground.

They continued to walk around the large town, or small city, depending how one would look at it. They went into several of the eateries but were turned away or refused by most. Molly was about ready to give up on finding a decent place to play when she heard something awfully curious.

"What's that?" Pepper asked her.

She looked around. "Why—I believe that it's fiddle music." They followed the sound until they came to a young woman playing a violin on a street corner, playing a slow, sad melancholy tune. A tin can was at her feet, for people to give a few pennies as they walked by.

The girl must have been about twenty-five or so, and her blonde hair hung into her dark face as she pulled the bow back and forth. The sight made Molly simmer, but she wondered where the strange feeling of jealousy was stemming from. But then Molly knew. She wanted to be the only act in town! No wonder she couldn't find anywhere to play.

The woman closed her song and pulled the violin from her chin; noticing Molly's dark frown and Pepper standing behind her.

"Is that a violin I see on your back?" the woman asked.

"No, it's a pair of wings," Molly answered.

The woman raised her eyebrows, but didn't retaliate. "Well, you seem like a sharp person that would be good at playing the fiddle. Do you care to play a duet?"

"What do you want me to play," Molly replied, "Melody or harmony?"

"You pick."

Molly took her violin case off her back and set it on the bench. She pulled out the violin and tightened the bow hairs, noticing the sun sinking on the horizon. People would be coming home from their job; if they had one, soon. Hopefully they would pass this way on their way home. She wanted people to see this.

"Harmony," she said arrogantly. She knew that it was harder.

The woman smiled. "How about an easy one, like the song 'Golden Slippers'?"

"No," Molly said, "I want the song 'Leather Britches'."

"Okay, will do," said the girl.

One, two, three, four!

They both began on four, and the competition between them ended up making the song intensely beautiful. Molly stopped at the end, but the other girl kept on going, so Molly put her violin up and kept on.

While all this was happening, Pepper somehow happened to slip away. Molly didn't even notice, as she was busy trying to win a fight. A fiddle fight.

After the second time, they both stopped. "Very good," the girl told Molly, "You're quite impressive. How did you learn?"

"Never mind you," said Molly, eager for there to be a clear winner in the fight. "What is the hardest song you can play? The best song?"

"You ask a hard question," said the girl, "I have lots of songs in my repotorie that I can choose from. Why don't you think of one first?"

Molly thought hard, but only for a second, hastily beginning to play "Cotton-Eyed Joe" a song her grandfather had taught her long ago.

Where did you come from?
Where did you go?
Where did you come from Cotton-eyed Joe?
If it hadn't of been for Cotton-eyed Joe, I'd been married long time ago!

Molly thought of the words in her head as she played. Faster and faster she went, until she completed the song with one last loud pull of her bow over the strings.

Clink!

Molly looked up and noticed that there were quite a few people passing by them, and some people were even crowded around her, clapping their hands. But what she first noticed that someone had thrown a nickel in the girl's tin can.

"Hey!" she thought aloud, "We're not a duet, I'm a soloist. That should be my money!"

"Sorry," the other girl said, "But it's in *my* tip can."

Clank! Molly heard another sound, but this time it wasn't money in the girl's jar.

"Thought this would come in handy," Pepper said after he set the large, slightly rusty, coffee can on the ground in front of where Molly stood, with a silly grin on his face.

"Yeah, you're going to need it," said the girl, "because; just like she said, we aren't a duet, we're Dueling Fiddles!!"

The small audience clapped and someone whistled. The blonde girl put the violin under her chin and played a song that Molly didn't know. It was a waltz, clear and wonderful, that sounded very hard. Molly ears strained to hear that it contained lots of sharps and flats, extra high fingerings and low ones.

The girl grinned when it was over. A couple of people threw some pennies in her can. Someone threw a piece of garbage. Molly frowned, wondering why people would be so inconsiderate at times.

She knew that people really didn't appreciate songs that were hard for fiddlers to play. She knew that they really liked songs that *sounded* hard to play, but most of the time weren't really. That's why Molly liked Boil the Cabbage so much. But Boil the Cabbage wouldn't do in this case. She needed something different.

She started out with a song called Liberty. Neither a hoedown or a waltz, it was somewhere in the middle, and people loved the song.

Pepper watched her play, he didn't say anything but Molly noticed his fingers moving anxiously as if he were holding an imaginary guitar.

Immediately after the song was finished, she ripped into the tune, "Devil's Dream". Up down up down up down. Her arm moved faster and faster as she began to play the tune. The second time. Down up down up down up. As long as she kept her head saying the down, up, pattern, she thought she could stick with it. 1, 2, 3, 2, 3, 2 ,3, 2. Keep your fingers numbered! She thought. The third time. Downupdownupdownupdownupdownup. DOWN DOWN!

She finished out the end of the song, sweating and breathing heavily. She couldn't believe how fast she'd played the song. Neither could the people standing around her or Pepper, apparently. Their mouths hung open wide.

They were speechless for a minute. But the blonde girl wasn't.

"No fair!" She yelled, "you played two songs!"

Quite a few pennies sailed into Molly's coffee can. A well-off young boy put in a nickel. But what really surprised her was when a man walked up right next to her and placed a fifty-cent piece in her palm. It felt heavy and out of place there, and Molly looked up at the man.

"I haven't heard anything like that for years," he said to her. "People aren't into playing these wonderful instruments anymore. Only a handful do. But you are the best I've ever heard. Ever."

He smiled enormously at her. "Oh, but there was one person I knew who was better than you," he said, and Molly's face fell slightly.

"But he passed away only a short time ago. He probably could have kept right up with you. He was my father."

The man put his hands into his pockets, and left. Molly had never seen him before, and she would never see him again.

"No fair!" the girl repeated angrily, and made her way over to Molly.

Pepper ran slyly under the girls' feet and grabbed the coffee can before either of the girls could do anything about it, holding his hand over the top of the can as he bolted away.

Molly wanted to say something smart back to the girl. She had played two songs, but she had played the first in regular time just to show the audience how fast she really could go. And she had blended the two together very effectively.

But all she could say was, "But it's in *my* coffee can." And she looked back to Pepper and grinned.

Chapter 4

They had no problem finding a place to sleep that night. Tons of people had seen the performance, and most were willing to allow them a place to stay if only Molly would play "Devil's Dream" one more time for their families before they all went to bed.

Molly sat in a warm room upstairs on a woven rug, holding the coffee can in her hand. Pepper sat on the other side of the rug, leaning back on his hands and grinning ear to ear. "Do you think we made enough?" he asked.

"I don't know," Molly said, and then dumped the contents of the can onto the floor.

"Dueling fiddles!" he said as he took a good look at the quarter. "I liked it. I wonder if we could do any more of those?"

Molly snatched away the quarter. "No. I don't think so. It's only once in a blue moon that I find another fiddle player, next to never a girl almost my age."

Truth was, Molly just now felt a twinge of regret for so offending the girl.

Pepper snorted. "Close to your age? She looked ten or fifteen years older." He paused for a minute. "Hey, you never did tell me how old you were."

"We have ninety-six cents." Molly interrupted, moving the pile toward him. "Not including the fifty cents that we had from before that."

"A whole dollar and forty-six cents!" Pepper exclaimed, "we could buy a nice guitar with that much."

Molly frowned slightly as she folded the money into her hankerchief and put it safely into the little compartment in her fiddle case. He seemed to be forgetting that he had done next to nothing to earning most of the money they had.

"Well, it's getting late. You should head out to the barn, Pepper. That's where these kind people have a place for you to stay."

They walked to the open door together and Pepper stopped. "Out in the barn. Uggh! That's not fair."

"Well, you will remember that I am the one that had entertained them tonight, as well as to help them make dinner and do dishes, so you deserve to sleep out in the barn!"

She started to shut the door. "Wait!" he said. Molly opened it a minute again.

"It isn't very nice being all alone. We both might get kinda lonely. Are you sure that you don't need someone to keep you warm in there?"

Molly groaned then responded by pushing him out and slamming the door in his face.

The pair set off early again the next morning. As they neared Chicago, they both decided it would be best to go around the city, and instead go through the smaller city of Wheaton. Pepper couldn't wait to get his hands on a guitar. Molly only hoped that he could actually play the instrument.

After a few days' travel, they entered the city. "We should look for a pawn shop or something like that," Pepper said. "That's where they'll have guitars for a decent price. Even if we did find an instrument shop, we wouldn't be able to afford one and they'd kick us out before we could even take a look."

"Yeah," Molly said, "Knowing the way you smell."

Pepper frowned. "Well, maybe we should wash up a little bit before we go into a store." Molly agreed.

A half hour later they entered the first used shop they came to, after cleaning up a bit in the restroom of a public building. Molly slipped on her faded skirt and combed her ratted hair into two braids. Pepper cleaned his face and combed out his hair, there was nothing he could do about his clothes as they were the only ones he owned.

"We'll have to see about getting you some new clothes," Molly told him. "Those ones are getting pretty grubby."

Pepper snorted, but didn't say anything.

"Really," Molly went on, "Look at those trousers! There at least four inches above your bare heels! And I do think we should get you some shoes."

"Aw, nobody ever noticed that I have bare feet unless they're lookin' to steal my shoes." Pepper told her.

They were both quiet when they came up to the door of the pawn shop. "Well, we could at least find some material to add onto those pants. You look quite ridiculous."

Inside the pawn shop was hot and the air smelled of pine wood and smoke. Stacks of old books lay on a shelf, kitchen pots and pans tucked away in a corner, men's tools in another. The place had nearly everything one could want, trinkets and toys, tools and materials, dishes and clothing.

The place was nearly vacant, except for an older man sitting behind a table in the middle of the room. He sat reading a faded newspaper, his laced up boots casually resting on top of his desk. He didn't stand, but eyed them suspiciously from over his paper as they looked at the items.

Pepper led Molly straight to the back room, where eight or nine guitars sat, some in stands and others resting against the wall or on a wooden bench.

Pepper uttered a low whistle. "Look at this one," he said, "I like it." He picked up a beautiful guitar and sat down in the folding chair, and strummed a chord. "Sounds right pretty, too."

He then glanced at the price tag hanging around the neck. "Twelve dollars!" he hollered, "I ain't paying no twelve dollars for that! Too much!"

"Shhhhh!" Molly chided him. "Be quiet. You know that he could kick us out."

She picked up a guitar that looked nice but had a few chips on the outside of the case. "Look at this one," she said, "It looks nice and I'm sure that it would be more affordable." She attempted to play something on it, but what came out was little more than a collection of jumbled notes.

Pepper laughed. "Here, let me see it," he said, "I'm the one who's going to be playin' it."

He strummed a chord, then frowned and messed with the tuning pegs a bit. He tried again.

"Oh my darlin' oh my darling, or my darling, Clementine;
  You are lost and gone forever, oh my darling, Clementine!"

"Shhh!" Molly told him again, "I think that the man is coming back here."

Pepper grinned, and said, "Don't say anything. I'll handle this. Just smile and nod."

Molly was confused, but didn't have time to ask him about it because the storekeeper suddenly entered the back room. "May I help you?" He asked, looking a little irritated.

Molly looked at his eyes through his round spectacles, and began to open her mouth to answer but Pepper spoke first.

"Well, yes you could," he said to the storekeeper. "My darling young wife here has just learned to play the gee-tar and she needs a reliable instrument to have for her own to play."

He hugged Molly from the side when he said that and Molly uncomfortably fought the urge to pull away. *He'd better know what he's doing,* she thought angrily.

"She's been saving up, (you know how tough times had been. Good golly!) and I even took a little bit of the bread money to put in her pot. She's been working hard, she has! She saw this little gee-tar that she really likes here for $2. But she hasn't got that kind of money! All these long months of back-breaking labor and she hasn't even gotten $2 yet."

The man still looked unsympathetic, but Molly watched for any signs of change.

Then Pepper put it out in the open. "I've seen that this instrument is in pretty tough shape. How about $1.25 for it?"

The man's eyes moved from Molly to Pepper, then back to Molly again. He scratched his moustache in thought. "I don't know," he finally said, "that is a lot less that what I'm asking for it."

He thought for awhile again, the room nearly silent. A fly buzzed around the light and the wooden floor squeaked beneath her as Molly shifted her weight uneasily.

"I think that I could possibly sacrifice it for $1.60."

Molly's face fell. Pepper looked downcast for a minute, but then said, "I'm sorry, but the girl only has $1.30. If you could give it to her for that much you know that the instrument would be well-used and taken care of."

The man shook his head, but Pepper sensed the hesitation. "Alright then," Pepper said, "I guess we'll be going now."

Pepper lead Molly toward the door, and whispered into her ear, "Keep it up!"

Molly looked even more depressed than she already did.

"Wait," the man called. The two looked back at him. "You know, times have been tough and I haven't sold one guitar for six months. I'm getting kind of sick of looking at them collecting dust. I think that I could give it to this young lady for $1.30. And I'll even throw in a case because I know she'll need one."

Molly was disgusted by the way Pepper so easily lied, but it was getting them a guitar for a good price. She smiled again. Pepper looked at Molly and winked, and she knew that they had it made.

They had left the city that afternoon, eager to get on with their traveling. Early that evening, they stopped to rest near a creek in a wooded area. The water running down the stream flowing over the rocks made a soothing noise, and Molly couldn't resist but to pull her skirt above her knees and go wading into the water.

She watched a couple of little fish dart around the bottom of the creek and deeply inhaled the fresh air. She was glad to be out of the city again. But the fish made her wonder where they were going to get their next meal.

Pepper sat with his lean back against the trunk of a solid tree, watching Molly with a smile on his face. The wind tugged at a loose piece of his rust-colored hair and his brown eyes sparkled as he called out, "Hey, Molly, get out that violin and let's do some jamming!"

Molly waded out of the creek reluctantly and grabbed her violin case that was sitting on the bank. She opened it up and pulled out her violin, ready to play. Pepper held the guitar in his lap, and looked at Molly. "Go ahead," he finally said, "pick a song."

"What songs do you know?" Molly asked, "so that you'll be able to play along with me?"

"It doesn't matter," he said, "any song you'd like."

Boil the Cabbage was a familiar song that Molly liked, so she started with that. Pepper closed his eyes and listened to the song for a minute, then came in with the guitar. He tripped over a few chords at first, but was playing like a pro in no time. Molly sped it up a little bit, and Pepper sped up his chords just as fast. They both stopped on the last note, grinning at each other.

"What'd I tell you?" Pepper said, "It sounds great, doesn't it?"

Molly had to admit that Pepper was right, it always sounded fine when she played alone but when she played with guitar it sounded amazing.

She began to play "Blackberry Blossom", another favorite song of hers, and Pepper played right along. Then Molly played another song. And another. Before she knew it, they'd been playing an hour and the sun was already beginning to signal that there wasn't much left of the day.

"Alright Pepper, we need to find a place to stay for the night," Molly said as she put her violin away. Pepper carefully laid the guitar in the case and looked up at her.

"We do have sixteen cents left. We could use that to get us a meal."

Molly felt extremely tired, and although she couldn't wait to try out their new act, she didn't feel like playing in a hotel or even doing dishes for her stay. Pepper looked at her tired face, and he could tell.

"Tell you what, we can get to the next town in a couple hours. If we use so much of the money we have left for our meal, we could put the rest of it toward a room for you, I'll clean out stalls tonight and the next morning and sleep in the barn at the livery stable or the owner's own barn. We sure would be able to make more money later."

Molly felt extremely grateful for Pepper's kind offer, but also a little confused. But she was too tired to ask him about it, so they walked on east toward the next town.

Molly loosened the hairs on her bow, and then carefully slipped it back into the velvety interior of her fiddle case. She shut the lid of the case and clicked it shut, then grinned at Pepper. He smiled back.

"Can you believe it?" She asked him. "People loved it! We were amazing! We didn't get a lot of money, but the surprising smiles on those sad faces were enough for me."

He picked up his guitar and nodded. "Yeah," he agreed with her.

The two started walking down a little dirt road that led out of the city. "I wonder what it would be like to be famous," he asked her as they walked. "I've seen pictures in magazines about how the movie stars live, and I tell you what! They live like royalty. No going hungry for them! They don't even have to eat plain ol' biscuits and gravy, they get to drink wine and eat steak and caviar every night!"

Molly didn't know what caviar was, nor did she care. "Such foolishness," she said, "half of our nation is going hungry and all that those pigs can think of is what they're having for their next meal."

Pepper tossed his long hair, but then combed it out a bit with the flat of his hand while looking at Molly. "Well, can you imagine it? One day we may even be well-known. Or even maybe we could be famous."

"Imagine that," Molly said, "the sad-eyed girl and redhead ragamuffin living in a giant mansion eating steak and caav-i-are."

"Aw, you wouldn't be so sad-eyed if you would smile every once in awhile, and not just when you're playing that fiddle. It would make you look a little older too," he told her, then playfully punched at her arm. Molly took both arms and shoved him off the road into the long prairie grass.

He climbed up the small ditch, laughing, and began to chase her to get her back. She dodged out of the way, then sped ahead. "Stop!" she giggled before he could get to her. "You can't get me back. You deserved that."

He complied and once again they walked calmly down the road. "We are almost to Jamestown," he informed her, "that is a good railroad city. I think that we could hop aboard a train heading east and save us walking a couple of states."

"Wait," Molly protested, "train-hopping is dangerous and illegal. They could throw us in prison for that. There's no way we're hopping on a train. We can make it all the way there on foot."

"We aren't foot-sore nags, Molly," he disagreed, "but that's what we will be by the time we get there. We have to hop a train if you plan on getting to New York before we grow old and die."

Molly frowned, thinking that Pepper was being quite a bit too dramatic. "Have you ever hopped a train?" she asked him.

"Once." Pepper said, "once when I was little, me and my brother hopped a train and rode it for two miles, 'fore they stopped at the next town and kicked us out. It seemed like a long way to walk back, but now it sure seems like nothing compared to all this walking."

"Well, you're inexperienced then," Molly poked at him. "I don't think we should."

"I'm more experienced than you," Pepper shot back, "and I think for once you should just close your mouth and listen to me, bossy. Now that you aren't a one-man show, you have some--if even just a little bit-- to lose here. I think that we should ride the rails, and I know that you will thank me for it later."

Molly felt hurt, but didn't come up with anything to shoot back at him. Her silence bothered Pepper, and he softened. "Mostly I think you should just trust me for once." Molly looked at him and nodded. An old blue pickup passed them by on the road, but then put on the brakes and abruptly stopped in front of them.

Pepper waved at the driver, then pulled down the tailgate and Molly hopped up beside him on the back of the truck. They rode in silence until they got to the next town.

The pair arrived at Jamestown within a couple of days. It was a bustling railroad town, with a railroad yard nearly in the exact center, with trains and other vehicles moving in and out nearly constantly.

Molly looked around, not knowing what to do or where to go. Pepper seemed much more confident. "We'll have to wait until the evening," he whispered into her ear. "That way it'll be harder for the cops to see us, and there's bound to be others hopping on the same train that can help us out."

He looked over to a large clock mounted on the side of a railroad building. "It looks like it's about noon now. That means we've got the whole afternoon to burn. What should we do?"

Molly looked around. "We don't have much money," she said, "but I really think that we need to buy you a new pair of trousers. You're starting to look quite ridiculous in those rags."

Pepper's face fell. "Clothes?" he asked, "I was thinking more like going out to get us some grub, then maybe going to a moving picture show or a horserace, if they have one."

Molly groaned. "You are such a kid," she said, "now act like an adult and help me look for a place to buy you something to wear."

They soon came upon a department store and made their way to the men's section. Molly sorted through racks of trousers and shirts until she found a few that she thought would fit Pepper. "Go into the fitting room and try these on to see if they fit," she told him.

He rolled his eyes. "Okay, mother."

He went into the fitting room and tried on the stacks of clothing that Molly had picked out for him. He came out with the pair he liked best, a sturdy pair of pants and a neat flannel shirt, and Molly nearly gasped.

"They look wonderful," she said, surprised at what a clean outfit could do for Pepper. "Now go put on your other clothes so that we can pay."

They began to make their way to the register. "Wait," Molly cried suddenly, "we still need to get you a pair of shoes."

Pepper looked down at Molly's own thinly clad feet and said, "Well, I think we should get you a new pair of shoes first. The ones you're wearing look like they're a hundred years old and they must pinch a bit."

"No, no." Molly said, "don't worry about my shoes. They are all just for the look of the thing, I don't need or desire shoes any more than you do."

Pepper shrugged. "Whatever you say."

They soon had found Pepper a pair of socks and durable boots and he laced them up around his feet before he left the department store.

"Well," Molly started, "we don't have a lot left but I do think we have enough to get us a nice meal. Let's go over to the corner café and get something to eat."

The meal had cost more than they thought it would. With all of the expenses of the day, all they had left were a few pennies after they had eaten their noon meal. They had spent almost all of the money that they had earned in the past week in less than a day.

"It's still only three o'clock," Molly sighed, exasperated.

Pepper looked over above her head across the street. He saw a tall, bright sign flashing with light that showed up even during the day. "We could go to the movies," he said.

"Pepper, we don't have enough money to go," she said disapprovingly.

"That's okay," he said, "we'll go anyway." He grabbed her hand and led her through a dark alley to the back of the building. Sure enough, there was a little sign on the top that had four large letters written across it: EXIT.

"A lot of these movie theatres still are too dumb to figure out to lock the door heading into the theatre. Or at least lock it from the outside. They still think that no one knows about these doors."

He turned the knob slowly and carefully and pushed the door open silently, pulling Molly in along with him. The theatre was pitch black, except for the large screen near the front of the giant room. The air smelled of buttery popcorn and other concessions, and even though Molly had just eaten, she felt herself drooling. No noise came from the screen, instead a piano player impressed the audience with his audible skill while the silent movie ran. An usher walked near to them, and Pepper pushed Molly and then himself flat against the wall so that they couldn't be seen.

He walked by, unnoticing, and Pepper brought Molly around to a front row seat. The theater was almost empty, Molly and Pepper were alone in that particular row, a few scattered people here and there in the seats was all that they saw.

Molly wanted to begin to enjoy the movie, but she noticed that Peppers hand still entwined her own. She didn't pull it away from him immediately, but looked at him, watching him smile eagerly at the screen and noticing the light reflecting in his eyes.

He leaned over to her, "You know, they say that they already have moving pictures with sound," he whispered into her ear, his short whiskers nearly touching the side of her face. "Can you imagine being able to hear people talk?"

She leaned back into her seat to watch the film. After awhile, Pepper pulled his hand away and then put it over her shoulder.

Alright, Molly thought to herself, *now you are going just a little too far.* She took his arm away from her body and put it into his own lap. "Keep your hands where they belong," she reminded him.

Pepper didn't say anything, but looked only a little embarrassed, so Molly settled down to enjoy the rest of the afternoon watching her "free" movie.

A full moon was out that night. Shadows moved silently in the darkness, stretching themselves out to be taller than life, then pulling down into short, fat little creatures. Crickets sang somewhere in the distance, once in awhile a loud rumble was heard from the moving rail cars. Most of the lights in town were out, some were dimmed slightly.

A tall lanky figure glided over the road heading out of town, along with a shorter figure that scrambled to keep up with the former. Pepper grabbed Molly's arm and pulled her over to hide behind a thick tree.

"See those guys over there?" He asked Molly, pointing to some tall, dark people in the distance. "They are conductors, don't let them catch even a sight of you. They have salt pellet guns and won't hesitate to shoot you right in the face."

"We have to wait until the train begins to move slightly. Then we'll know that everybody's inside, and if we can find an open boxcar we won't have any problems hopping in. You're a fast runner, right?"

"Try me," Molly answered. Even though her stomach churned uneasily with anticipation, if there was one thing she knew, it was how to run, and how to run fast.

They waited until the train chugged a big puff of black smoke, then made a loud clinking noise as it set off. Pepper waited for a second, then sprang ahead toward the train.

This will be easy, Molly thought, *the train's only moving at a snail's pace.* Molly burst forth from behind the tree, right on Pepper's heels.

Well, it looked to be moving at a snail's pace. The reality was that it was going faster. *Much faster,* Molly thought as she pumped her legs as fast as she could to get to the open boxcar. She ran beside the car for a few seconds waiting for Pepper to catch up. She made a grab at the end of the boxcar floor, but missed.

Pepper overcame her with his long legs and grabbed the ledge and made a swing at the car. He leaped into the moving car with a single jump. More smoke leaked from the front of the train and the whistle moaned ahead in the distance. *Click, clack, click clack!* The train's wheels kept on clicking faster and faster. Molly breathed heavily, struggling to keep up with the train.

She hoped and prayed that she wouldn't trip in the pitch black darkness. She knew it would be over if she did. She pulled her violin case off her back and threw it up to Pepper. He caught it and pulled it up into the train.

"Here, grab my hand," Pepper called out to her, "I'll help you up."

Molly lunged at his outstretched arm. He grabbed her and then pulled her up, both of them falling backwards onto the floor of the boxcar. Breathing heavily, they stared out at the rushing ground just outside. Molly's eyes were wide with something like fear; Pepper wasn't afraid but only a little shaken.

They sat like that for a moment, before they noticed a couple of men and a boy sitting in the corner of the boxcar. They all wore ratty clothing and sat in a little pile of leftover grain. Molly hurriedly climbed out of Pepper's lap and dusted herself off. She noticed the younger boy eyeing the instruments that were still laying on the floor of the boxcar. She opened her mouth to tell him to back off but was interrupted by Pepper.

"Oliver!" He exclaimed happily. "How did you get here?"

Molly looked from the boy, Oliver, to Pepper, and back to the boy. She wasn't sure what was going on. Oliver stood up. "Pepper!" he acknowledged.

As the boy stood up, Molly noticed that he wasn't even really a boy. He was a young man. He was clean shaven, with dark hair that was well kept. He had blueish-gray eyes that reflected the moonlight that brightened the small boxcar.

"How did you get here?" Pepper was asking. Oliver walked over to the side of the car where they stood.

"I'm heading east to see if I can I can find my great-aunt. I've heard that she still has money left."

"We're going east to--" Pepper stopped. "Wait, let me introduce you to Molly, my friend, a musician and a fine lady," he joked.

Molly frowned. Oliver nodded a little to acknowledge her. "Nice to meet you," he greeted. Pepper started talking again, but then stopped.

"Jeez, that reminds me Oliver, whatever did you do with your banjo?"

"Right here," he said as he pulled the banjo out from behind himself. "It's all I have left."

Molly smiled and her eyes lit up with excitement. A banjo! What an excellent addition to their instruments.

"I'd pull it out and we could play a few tunes, but you know how these conductors and guards are, they don't seem to appreciate it as much as we do," he said with a wink. "You still play that guitar, right?" he asked Pepper, "and I see that you've finally gotten yourself one."

Pepper grinned and puffed up a little. "We bought it, too, we didn't steal it."

"And what do you have in that little case of yours, Miss Molly," Oliver asked her. Molly instinctively pulled the case a little closer.

"I have a fiddle," she explained to him, "it was actually my grandfather's."

Oliver smiled a little broader. "Where are you heading to?" he asked, "are you riding this little train all the way over to Ohio or are you going to risk hopping back off?"

"We'll stay up here for the entire ride, for sure," Pepper said. "Where do you plan on heading after that?"

"Well, my aunt lives in North Carolina. I think I'm going to head that way."

Pepper's face fell a little. "How far is this train going into Ohio?"

"I think we might go as far as the middle of the state, but I'm not sure." Oliver guessed.

"Well, you could travel east on foot with us a little bit, and join our little pair to make it a trio," he told Oliver. "We don't make a lot of money, but we have enough to live without our stomachs growling and it's lots of fun."

Oliver grinned. "I think I could. I would like that."

Molly looked over to the two men who were still on the other side of the boxcar. One of them was asleep and snoring loudly. The other sat against the wall of the boxcar, with his hands in his pockets and his face staring blankly out into the moonlight. Both were unshaven and stank like old food. Molly shivered. This was definitely a time when she was glad to have Pepper along with her. Maybe he really would come in handy to have around.

The two boys continued to talk until Molly pulled out her blanket and laid it onto the floor. She curled up in a little ball on her blanket with her violin case still strapped to her back, and was soon sound asleep. The train movement gently rocked her like a baby in a cradle, and she slept so soundly that she didn't even notice when Pepper carefully pulled the violin case off her back and put it with the other two instruments, then sat beside them, guarding his two sleeping friends and their instruments late into the night.

Chapter 5

When the morning sunrise shot long warm fingers of light that stretched across her face through the slats in the boxcar, Molly awakened. She sat up in the boxcar, and groped for her fiddle case, which she found quickly. She sighed with relief, but the relief wasn't to last long. The two men were gone, and Oliver and Pepper were too.

The train came to a stop, and the large sliding door of the boxcar clicked. Molly pulled it open, ready to jump out into the city. What she saw surprised her.

The sun nearly blinded her as she opened the door. She didn't see the bustling activity of a railroad town. Or even anything ahead in the distance. The train stood still in the middle of a flat empty prairie, the short patches of grass swaying gently in the wind.

Her gaze fell to a small shack and a rusty windmill in distance. She climbed down from the boxcar, and made her way over to the all-too familiar little house. She went to the back of the building, where there was one small, dark window that she could look into.

She wiped dust from the surface, then looked into the house. She saw a table with five empty chairs around it. And old cookstove with a pot of water on its surface. Jackets neatly hung in the corner of the room on pegs. Everything in the house was covered with a thin film of dust, but she noticed that there were no people inside.

The slamming of the front door made her jump.

"Damn girl's run off,"

Molly hid behind the corner of the building and was surprised to see her father, a tall man with gray hair, who was wearing overalls and a thin shirt that made him look bigger than he actually was. He wiped his mouth on his sleeve, leaving a large white mark in the middle of his dust-covered face. He stormed down the yard, Molly's mother following close behind.

"Henry, you know she never liked it out here." She was nearly sobbing as she talked to Molly's father. Her father walked over to the barn, opened the door to go inside and was soon throwing in small amounts of grain to the animals. Molly still followed them, being careful not to let either of them see her.

Her mother continued, "She didn't like anything about farming this desolate god-forsaken land, she didn't like being so far away from any neighbors, and she didn't like starving."

Her father stopped and raised his thin frame to look down into his wife's eyes. "You think she's doing any better now?" he asked angrily. "I'd bet that stupid girl's stomach is twisted with hunger even more now than it had ever been when she was here."

Her mother didn't say anything back, but Molly noticed the tears running down her cheeks. She took a step, intending to talk to her parents. But she stopped suddenly when she heard a loud rushing noise that sounded like the whirl of a hundred tornados. Molly turned her head slowly.

In the distance, a huge black cloud was rolling over the prairie, making a loud rushing sound as it blew toward the house. Her eyes widened with fear and her body froze in place.

Her parents ran out of the barn and noticed it too.

"Quick! Shut up the barn! Make sure all the animals are inside," her father was calling out frantically.

"Thomas! Marshall! Get the rags and soak 'em with water!" her mother called out to her brothers.

Molly wished that she could run around and help, as she did so many times before, but she still seemed to be paralyzed with fear. Only when the family ran into the house did she realize that she had to get in too or she would die.

She ran to the door and pounded on it with all her might. "Ma! Pa! Let me in! Please!" The air was rushing even louder now as the topsoil from Colorado or Kansas moved toward the little shack, and the coarse dirt was already beginning to cut into her skin. Her family would never be able to hear her.

"Let me in! Let me in—"

"MOLLY! Molly!"

Molly felt herself being shaken softly.

"Molly! You are already in."

She opened her eyes and noticed Pepper in front of her with a worried look on his face. She sat up in the boxcar, which was still rumbling along at its steady pace. She rubbed her aching head and looked around her, noticing that the two men were gone and only Oliver, Pepper and herself were in the car.

"What kind of a dream were you having, Molly? You sounded worse than an old coyote with a thorn in his foot. Are you alright?" Pepper looked concerned.

"I'm okay. I was just having a nightmare. A very realistic nightmare."

Click, clack, clickity, clack. The railroad car continued on with its rollicking rhythm. "We should be stopping in a couple of hours," Oliver told them. "We've already crossed the Ohio state line."

Sure enough, a couple of hours later the train came to a halt just outside of a town. "Quick," Pepper whispered harshly, "open the car door, then we'll all jump out together and run for cover before they can nail us."

Oliver and Pepper opened the car door, and the three jumped out with their instruments held above their heads to keep them safe. Then they all ran for it. With a bounding gait, Molly was able to keep ahead of the boys until she got to cover. She heard a shout from a couple of men behind her near the railcar, but she didn't look back and just went on running.

She safely met Pepper and Oliver a little ways off. "So how was your first train-hopping experience?" Pepper asked.

"Not as bad as I thought it would be," Molly admitted. "But where are we going now?"

"There's only one way to keep going, and that's east."

"I think that we could do a performance in the little town that's coming up," Oliver said, "hopefully they'll be starving for some good entertainment."

The three set off, Pepper and Oliver leading the way with Molly following close behind.

They arrived in the town in the late afternoon, all three of their stomachs growling hungrily. The town was a pleasant one, with houses neatly tucked into the neighborhood, with sun-baked white wooden fences crisscrossing around the perimeters of the yards. Molly heard some chickens clucking and crowing in the backyards of some, and knew that these people were having just as hard a time as the rest of the nation was.

"Do you think we should do a tin-can performance, or should we actually try to land us a little gig?" Oliver asked as he looked around at the neighborhood they were crossing through.

Before Pepper could open his mouth Molly answered. "I think that we could do both." She gestured toward a park ahead in the distance. There was a simple swing set there, and a large open gazebo in the center of the park with benches around it. The park seemed to be in the near middle of the town, the perfect place for entertaining.

"It's early enough so that we could do a quick performance here, then we could go to a little restaurant for supper entertaining. Even if no one is watching, it would be a good place to have a little practice."

Pepper and Oliver agreed. They made their way to the gazebo and each of them got their instrument ready. Pepper sat down with his guitar, Oliver cinched up his banjo so that he could stand and Molly held her bow ready.

"I think we should practice for a little while, first," Molly advised. "It would help us to sound better when we really start and it would attract people."

Pepper nodded and started moving his fingers in a three-chord progression. Oliver began to pick his strings in some sort of interesting order, and harmonized perfectly with Pepper. Sunlight filtered in on the two boys and made them squint, but the park was still quiet except for the assortment of singing birds. Molly scratched the top of her head with the tip of her bow and thought for a minute.

The chord progression was a common one, but she couldn't think of the song to go with it. She snapped her fingers. That was it! She began to play the melody. Oliver shook his head, trying to get the dark piece of hair that was hanging in his eyes back to where it belonged without taking his hands off his banjo. He kept on playing the harmony, and there was a huge smile on his face when he heard Molly jump in.

She is good, he thought to himself, but didn't say anything as he kept on picking notes. Molly played through the song again and then stopped and began to sing.

As I was goin' down the road,
With a tired team and heavy load,
I cracked my whip and the leader sprung,
I says hey to the wagon tongue!

Turkey in the Straw, turkey in the hay!
Turkey in the straw, turkey in the hay,
Roll 'em up and twist 'em up high tuck-a-haw,
And hit 'em up with a tune called Turkey in the straw!

Molly played again, but when she started at the chorus again Oliver suddenly started playing the melody. Her bow scratched with a sudden stop, and Pepper looked over curiously at her.

Oliver continued to play the melody while Molly paused for a minute. He opened his mouth wide and began to sing the second verse of the song:

Oh I went out to milk and I didn't know how,
I milked a goat instead of a cow,
A monkey sittin' on a pile of straw
A winkin' at his mother-in-law!

Molly quietly moved the bow on her fiddle until she found the harmony and moved more into the background of the music. It was the first time that she had ever played the other part of the song in her life. But the more she experimented, the more she got it figured out, so that by the last time the chorus was played she was able to do it perfectly.

Molly put her instrument at her side and sang it again, with Oliver and Pepper joining in as an amazing three-part tune.

Turkey in the straw, turkey in the hay!
Roll 'em up and twist 'em up a high tack-a-haw
And hit 'em up with a tune called

TURKEY IN THE STRAW!

They all stopped promptly on the same note.

"Yee Haw!" Pepper hollered, "We sound great! I'm sure glad we found you Oliver."

Molly looked down below them in the park and noticed three young kids sitting on the benches, watching with their mouths gaping open. Two of them began to clap excitedly, while the other one stood up and left.

"Oh well," said Oliver, watching the kid get up and leave. "We can't please everyone."

Molly smiled at the children and took a quick little bow, making them clap even more. She turned to Oliver and Pepper. "Let's do another one," she said, grinning.

The three played Boil the Cabbage, Angus Campbell, Black Velvet Waltz and Blackberry Blossom before they noticed all of the people in the park below. Most of the people had come from the ride home and had stopped to listen for a minute or two. Everyone loved free entertainment. There were so many people that they hardly could believe their ears when they heard the tremendous amount of clapping and cheering, even a whistle thrown in every once in awhile.

There were so many people that there wasn't even enough room on all the benches, and many of them were standing on the grass. They gazed at Oliver, Pepper and Molly with gratitude and admiration in their eyes. A few of the men watching even made an attempt at a sort of wild square dance, causing most of the people to hoot with laughter.

Molly smiled genuinely the entire time, and Pepper made her day when he pulled her aside and whispered in her ear, "Don't get too much of a big head. You're not famous yet, but I can tell that you must be really happy with all this. Even your eyes are smiling."

Pepper was against sleeping in the town for the night, pointing out that if anyone recognized them from the train that they could be thrown in jail.

"Na," said Oliver, "we shouldn't have to worry too much about getting thrown in jail. Unless we were real trouble makers, it'd cost them too much to feed us in prison."

"Besides," Molly said, "we have enough money to sleep very comfortably tonight. We should see if we could play in the hotel in town. That way maybe we could get a meal and a room for a good price."

The three tiredly walked into the nearest hotel that they could find. The place was beautiful, with colored rugs and beautiful light fixtures, but the lobby seemed to be empty. They heard people eating in the dining room, and began to make their way over to where they heard the cheerful din.

"Hey!" someone called to them. Molly stopped in her tracks. There was no way that they could be kicked out already!

"Yes," Pepper squared himself up and answered to a man that was walking out from behind the desk in the lobby.

"Were you kids the ones who played in the park today?" he asked.

"Sure are."

"Would you consider playing in our dining room tonight?"

Molly could hardly believe her ears. Someone was asking her to play in their building! Pepper and Oliver looked at her in anticipation. She barely opened her mouth to speak when someone else entered the room.

"Excuse me!"

It was a woman who had just entered the building. She wore a neat blouse and skirt with high heels and a bright palette of makeup on her face.

"I saw your group in the park. I just have to have you perform at our ladies meeting and dinner tonight! I would be willing to pay you some."

Oliver's and Molly's mouth hung open in surprise.

"Wait a minute! Wait a minute!" The man started again. "I was just drafting them to play in our dining room tonight, I asked them first so I get them! And if there's money involved," he paused to pull out his wallet from his back pocket. "I'll give them $3 cash to perform. And I say that's pretty lucky for some dirty kids who just started out."

"Five dollars!" the lady said, "I'm sure you would love to get five whole dollars for something you folks probably just love to do anyway."

Molly began to nod, but Pepper squinted and just scratched his chin. "Hmm," he said, "I don't know if we can do that. We could have plenty of other arrangements made tonight."

A small crowd was beginning to gather in the lobby of the hotel, wondering about the discussion that was occurring. Many of them, Molly recalled, had been at the park.

"I'll give them five dollars and fifty cents." The man said again.

"No, no!" interrupted Pepper. "All this fighting. Two dollars! Five-fifty! No, we already have a set price and we will only perform for ten dollars cash."

Ten dollars! Molly gasped inwardly Who could afford ten dollars, more than two weeks pay for the average family?

"Oh, plus room and board," Pepper added with a grin.

Apparently the woman had a solid job with plenty of money to spare, because she pulled out a crisp ten-dollar bill, determined to have them perform for her. Pepper eyed the bill greedily.

"But first you'll have to wash up," she told them. "And if you really are travelers with no home, I'll let you use my own personal bathroom."

The three agreed to the bath. The woman walked out the door, smiling haughtily and glancing at the other man though the corners of her eyes.

Pepper, Oliver and Molly followed after her through the small crowd, listening to the click, click of her high heels the whole way.

After they went outside, the woman led them to her car, a shining, just-waxed looking Ford. "Hop in, kids," she told them. Molly couldn't wait. She hadn't ridden in a real car for as long as she could remember, although she had ridden in the back of many a pickup, she didn't consider that a real car ride.

The three eagerly climbed aboard, ready for whatever new adventure would await them.

Two days later they were walking away from the town with fourteen dollars and eighty cents stuffed inside the compartment of

Molly's fiddle case. They had played for the woman's meeting and dinner, receiving many wonderful compliments and encouragement all around from the women and men who had attended. Pepper, Oliver and Molly could hardly believe their good luck.

They had even considered staying in the town for a little longer, but Oliver pointed out that they needed to keep the people wanting more, and Molly and Pepper agreed.

Now the three continued on their journey east. They were nearing the branch where Oliver would have to leave. They continued to walk down a worn dirt road, when Oliver noticed a sign pointing out where they were.

"Only about ten more miles I can travel with you," he said with a hint of disappointment in his voice.

Molly and Pepper's faces were both downcast as they continued to walk along the road. The threesome made an interesting sight. Long and lanky Pepper wore his nice clothes and looked quite presentable but his hair continued to grow longer until it was almost draping down his neck, much to Molly's disgust.

Oliver's dark hair, on the other hand, was cut short and he wore a newsboy hat over it. His banjo was hung by a thick piece of twine over his shoulder; and he walked with both his hands stuffed into the pockets of his trousers.

Molly walked right beside them, her hair and her skirt blowing gently around her. She wore a surly look on her face and didn't smile much, her bare feet were beginning to ache but she refused to complain out loud.

"We should start looking for a place to stay," Pepper announced shortly.

"I don't know if we'll be able to, there's no town for five miles and if we don't find a farmstead to stay at we'll have to camp out tonight." Oliver said. Molly looked to the west and noticed that it was nearly dusk, and she picked up her pace a bit.

The three headed off the road a bit after that and headed in a slightly different direction. The trees were beginning to get rather thick, but they were sure that they would be able to find a farmstead soon, or at least a nice place to make camp.

"Look!" Pepper said, "There's a light up ahead, we must be getting closer to someone's place."

They continued on with more energy, eager to get a place to rest. But when they got closer, they suddenly noticed that the light wasn't exactly what they thought it to be, it looked more like a campfire.

"Let's approach slowly," Oliver said, "we don't know for sure who it could be."

They came quite close to the clearing when they noticed about a dozen men standing in white robes and hoods. A few of the men wore the hoods over their faces to hide their identities, but most of them had the hoods flung back casually. The three hid behind some tall bushes and looked in, and saw what appeared to be a thick burning cross, about six feet high. One man stood out from the rest and talked to the other men.

Molly was puzzled. "We should get out of here," she said, "I don't know what they're doing but it doesn't look friendly and I don't think strangers are invited."

"No," Pepper whispered excitedly, "I know what it is, it's the KKK! The Klu Klux Klan."

He received blank looks from Oliver and Molly.

"You know," he continued, "those people, or that secret club that you always hear about but never see. The ones that do stuff to blacks and Catholics and such." He turned to watch closer. "I don't know what they do for sure, but I want to find out. It looks kind of interesting."

Oliver didn't agree. "No, we don't want them to find us. If what they're really doing is secret, then they won't want us around. Let's just get going and they'll never notice we were here."

"Let's just stay for a little while," Pepper begged, still watching the meeting.

Oliver and Molly gave each other knowing looks, but didn't say anything. Molly guessed that they could stay for a little while.

Molly didn't pay much attention, she was too tired to notice much that was going on. She watched for awhile, watching the men stand straight and erect, seemingly paying close attention to every word of their leader. She heard the men in hoods talk about FDR, and about how certain policies would affect their livelihood, about a new black moving into the community. It disgusted her, she felt like it was just a bunch of boys wanting to have a secret club was all, they didn't seem like they would accomplish much.

Molly leaned against a tree and closed her eyes, barely noticing Pepper climb up into one of the trees to get a better look. Oliver knelt in the bushes, still watching them. Pepper snaked up the tree even farther until he leaned out of one the branches nearly right above where the men were having their meeting. She looked up at him, amazed at how childlike he looked up there, a glimmer of moonlight illuminating the top of his carrot-top hair. She looked down his too-short trousers and saw his dirty bare feet grasping the branch. She noticed Oliver slowly part the bush he was hiding behind to get a better look. Molly closed her eyes again, thinking to herself. *We're going to get in trouble. We're going to get in trouble!* Her heart beat a little faster.

Oliver squirmed a little to get more comfortable and didn't realize that he had caught one of his banjos strings in a branch, and it pulled out with a loud *PING* as the string left the instrument.

Molly's eyes snapped open and somehow Pepper managed to fall out of the tree at exactly the same time, landing a terrible belly-flop right into the clearing where the men stood.

There was no doubt that they had heard the noise of Oliver's banjo, and Molly jumped to her feet, her eyes wide with fear. She blasted out at a run to reach Pepper, when Oliver grabbed her arm in an iron-like grip. His eyes turned and he glanced at Pepper, who had been surrounded by the men but was gesturing frantically at Oliver, telling him to run.

"Quick!" he said to Molly, "We have to get out of here!"

Molly could hardly believe what they were doing, but had enough sense to whisper harshly to Oliver, "Grab Pepper's guitar!"

Oliver grabbed the guitar and pulled Molly away at a dead run, back toward the shelter of the trees.

Chapter 6

Molly's face was downcast as she walked along with Oliver on the road once again. She kept the violin on her back and carried Pepper's guitar case by the handle, a sad reminder of a missing person.

"What are we going to do?" she asked Oliver, "Can we go look for him? Do you think that we'd be able to find him? What on earth would they do with him?"

"Pepper can take care of himself," Oliver answered. "We'll never be able to find him, and besides, what's the worst they could do? Throw him in jail? It's not like they're going to lynch him."

Molly didn't know. The way those men had looked, all dressed up, she wondered if maybe they wouldn't string him up. Or maybe his smarty mouth and bad attitude would make them lynch him up anyway, Molly cheered herself up with a little humor. Though she had to admit that Pepper could talk himself out of almost anything if he set his mind to it.

"We'll go into town and stay there for awhile. Pepper will be back here with us as soon as he gets a chance to get away, and if he doesn't I'd still be confident that he is alright. That Pepper, he's a fighter if I ever saw one. And if he did get away from them and didn't come back, he would just move on. He's a drifter, just like the rest of us, and doesn't always want to settle down and tie any strings or tight connections with anybody."

Surprisingly, Molly found herself much more grieved then she thought she would be. Her thoughts swirled around what Oliver had just said as they continued to walk until they got to the next town.

One week later, Pepper still wasn't back. Oliver had picked up Pepper's guitar and had played it just as well as the banjo, and the pair spent a lot of their time holding performances.

The town was a kind one, and they spent most of their nights in various houses. Oliver had shown Molly how to read the hobo signs that were scratched into the fence posts or into an inconspicuous place on the side of the house. She didn't remember all of them, but made an effort to memorize the more important ones: a picture of a cat scratched into a fence post meant that there was a kind lady who lived in that house, a circle with two parallel arrows meant to get out fast, because travelers were not welcome in the area, and three diagonal lines meant that the place wasn't safe. Some of the signs made Molly think of Pepper.

The longer Pepper was gone, the more Molly seemed to miss him. She would often think of the funny little things he said or did, and how he had made her life so much more interesting. Pepper had just made such an amazing friend, it wouldn't be like him to leave and never come back. No, if Pepper had a chance to make his way back to Oliver and Molly, surely he would take it.

Two weeks passed. Oliver and Molly had just finished playing for the noon meal in a small Café, and as Oliver put away Pepper's guitar he confronted Molly.

"I don't think Pepper's coming back," he said quietly.

Molly loosened the strings on her bow and then put it in her case silently.

"I know that he's alright." Oliver said.

Molly sighed. Somehow she knew it too. Pepper would always be able to take care of himself. But why wouldn't he come back?

"I need to head down to Carolina now. I've waited as long as I can on the kid. I don't have any other options right now, but you have two: You can come with me, if you'd like. My aunt was always extremely kind, she would probably take you in and you'd have a great place to live until you decide to strike out on your own again. Or you could head off towards New York all on your own." He half-heartedly smiled, and Molly looked away.

"I'm going to keep on toward New York," she said quietly. It had always been her plan all along, ever since she had run away from home she had planned to go a big city and try to make money becoming a serious musician. She wasn't about to change her mind now.

Oliver heaved a heavy sigh and ran a hand through his dark hair. "I know that you've been on your own before, and now I can't stop you from going off again." He handed her Pepper's guitar and Molly looked down at the guitar case, a symbol of the person that was now missing from their group. Molly grabbed the guitar and then Oliver stretched out his hand to shake hers.

She put down the guitar and gave him a big hug. "Thank you so much, Oliver. You've been a ton of help."

They headed out on the street traveling together for a little way longer, until their ways split. They said their goodbyes once again and then Molly headed one way, going north, and Oliver the other, southward.

"Wait," she said quickly. Oliver stopped and turned around. Molly opened her violin case and pulled out six dollar-pieces. "You deserve more than this," she said and pressed it into his hand.

"I can't take it--" He started, but the way Molly looked so intently at him made him stop. Oliver smiled at her and took the money from her hand, then turned and headed away.

Molly had barely started walking the other way when she broke down into tears.

As Molly walked down the road the next day, she really began to feel the guitar weighing her down. What could she do with it? Until she could-- *if* she could-- find someone else who played guitar, she would be carrying the extra weight for no reason. The wind blew softly through the trees on either side of her and played with the tips of the prairie grass that grew in between. Even the clouds moved slowly across the bright blue sky, huge masses of fog that seemed so far away, yet close enough to touch. She raised her head as she heard the soft whine of an insect, then a loud chirp from another cricket. Life seemed so quiet when she was on her own. She didn't remember it being this quiet when she had traveled alone in the past, and wondered why.

She considered giving the guitar away, pawning it, or even leaving it somewhere where she would be able to find it later. She pondered about it and her thoughts soon led her back to Pepper.

Why did she feel this way anyway? She had always been content to be out on the open road by herself, and she had convinced herself that she didn't need anyone. It felt as if every time she allowed herself to get close to someone, they disappointed and let her down. Molly had learned the hard way not to put herself out there; to allow herself to be vulnerable to the whims of someone else; the capriciousness of someone else's feelings. Molly knew how selfish people could truly be. But Pepper seemed different. He had really seemed to care about her. Sure he was goofy and annoying, but he was a lot of help, and, she admitted, her best friend.

That's it, she thought to herself, *I have to go back and at least try to find him.*

And with that she turned herself around and began walking back toward the town.

No sooner had she made up her mind to go and find him when the opposite occurred. She felt as if she was being followed, her eyes danced back and forth as she tried to locate anyone that would be following her. She felt especially vulnerable now that she was alone. She tried to ignore it, but there was no denying that Molly could feel a presence.

She finally whirled, annoyed, looking for the person that would dare to bother her so much. She nearly jumped out of her skin and then she dropped the guitar when she felt a tapping on her shoulder from behind.

"Pepper!" she gasped.

Chapter 7

He grinned the same silly grin of his, and she exhaled with relief. But she noticed that he had his hair cut and was wearing some rather nice-looking clothes.

Molly couldn't contain herself, she reached up to wrap her arms around his neck in a giant hug. Pepper looked away awkwardly until she pulled away.

"Where have you been?" she asked.

"Geez, you seem just a little worried about me," he kidded her in his deep voice.

Molly frowned and threw his guitar toward him. "Take this," she said, "and tell all."

"I was only a little worried when they surrounded me," Pepper exaggerated, starting a story. "I didn't think they were going to do anything too horrible to me.

"They brought me to someone's house and locked me upstairs in a bedroom and then debated on what to do with me. The next morning two men and a woman brought me downstairs and gave me a stern lecture about not getting into other people's business, but I didn't listen much to them.

"They made me do some farm chores but I didn't have any chances of escaping. They treated me pretty well, they gave me good clothes and meals, and trimmed up my hair some, and took me to church on Sunday. But the next day they were supposed to take me to a central place for the CCC-the Civilian's Conservation Corps- and leave me there. They said that it wasn't good for a man, much less a kid, to be wandering around without employment or a family business to work in.

"I was curious as to just what I'd be doing. I learned that the CCC was a place for boys and tramps like me, a place where they could put us to work and give us a little money for it. It sounded okay, but when I heard that they were taking us to Kentucky to work on some park there, I balked. Hey, I didn't want to travel so far away against my will to something I would probably hate anyway.

"I didn't let them on to it right away. They were taking me there in their automobile, but when we stopped for gas I hopped out quick as lightning and hopped aboard a moving pickup that was heading the other direction before they even noticed.

"But not so fast as to forget this," he said, and pulled out a little wad of money, about twenty dollars. Molly gasped.

"Where'd you get that?"

"Ripped it off."

When Molly understood what he said, she began to scold him, but it was hard for her to do it with such a big smile on her face and they both ended up laughing out loud.

They set off on their way yet again. They were entering Pennsylvania now, getting closer than ever to New York. Through every town they passed through they had at least one performance, and though people everywhere had less money now than ever, Molly and Pepper seemed to make a little bit at each stop.

Towns began to get closer in between, and farmsteads became more scarce. There was hardly ever a time when Molly and Pepper had to sleep outdoors anymore.

"Darn!" Pepper said as he looked at the sun setting in the west. "I hoped that we would be able to get to the next town before the sun sets. It looks like we may be camping out tonight."

Molly looked away but continued to walk beside Pepper. She had hoped so too. The two continued to walk until they came to a small running stream.

"We could stay here tonight," Molly said, looking across the green field where they would be able to sleep. "I need to wash some of my clothes." Since they had been making money, Molly and Pepper had been able to afford two outfits and a pair of shoes each, and Molly hadn't washed her skirt for awhile yet.

Pepper set his guitar down on the grass and Molly gingerly set her violin next to it. She opened the little bag that she had for personal things and pulled out her skirt and a pair of socks, then the bar of laundry soap.

"You need to polish your shoes, Pepper," she told him before she went down to the bank of the creek. The water ran cool and clear and Molly couldn't resist dipping her hands into it for a drink. It was such a beautiful place to stay. She was glad that they had gotten there before sundown, she didn't want to do her chores the next morning.

Pepper sighed and dug out his shoes, then a little jar of polish out of the bag and set to work. Molly began sudsing her dirty skirt in the water, washing it carefully to prevent any more tears from forming. It was such a beautiful day, she could almost sing right there!

A pair of trousers were flung beside her. "Can you wash these up for me, Molly?"

Molly frowned at being so suddenly interrupted from her thoughts, and grabbed the trousers off the bank irately. The trousers flew back across the ground and smack into Pepper's face.

"Wash them yourself. I'm not your maid."

Pepper pulled the trousers off in surprise, but didn't say anything and continued with his shoe polishing. The sun sank lower into the sky until it disappeared over the horizon. Molly rolled out her bedroll and then slowly began to brush her hair.

"Hey, Molly!" Pepper called. "Come over here!"

Molly sighed, then dropped her comb. Pepper was sitting on the riverbank on a small hill. "Come sit next to me," he said, and gestured for her to sit. Molly plopped down beside him.

 "Look real close at all those lighting bugs above the river," he said quietly. Molly looked over and gasped, amazed by the vast number of the glowing bugs lighting up the night sky.

"You know," he said suddenly, "we've been together for a long time. Almost three months now." Molly looked at his face and into his eyes that were lit up by the light of the full moon. There was a sort of awkward silence as they both peered into each other's eyes, and Molly fought the urge to pull away from his gaze

Molly broke it by saying sarcastically, "But that doesn't mean that I have to wash your clothes."

Pepper burst into laughter. "You're such a sweet girl."

"Thanks."

"But really," he said. "You are so amazing. Before I met you I wouldn't listen to a thing anyone said and I saw my life kind of wasting away. I was doing all kinds of terrible things and getting into so much trouble. But when I first laid eyes on you I was mesmerized. You're such a tomboy, but really, you're beautiful."

Molly didn't know what to think about Pepper's sudden expressed emotion and she sat quietly and gazed over the creek until he spoke again.

"Sometimes it seems like we don't like each other at all. We fight a lot. We act immature." Molly glared at him. "Yes, even you," he finished.

Molly opened her mouth to retort "But you--"

Pepper interrupted her and whispered, "But I know you like me too."

He ran his finger down the bridge of her nose, smiling when he allowed her to do so without pulling away. And with that, he leaned down to kiss her.

At first it seemed Molly fought the urge to suddenly reel back, but after a few seconds she felt every bit as good and confident about it as Pepper did, so then moved her body closer to his, wrapped her arms around his neck and kissed him back.

Chapter 8

The next day things seemed a little bit changed between Molly and Pepper. Though the kissing was as far as they went, they did seem to care a little more for each other, and they fought less each day. On they went determinedly toward New York, though they didn't know what they would find there, they refused to let go of the hope that they would be able find *something* there.

They continued on foot, somewhat because they could make money playing in the towns along the way and partially because Molly refused to take any more risks riding the rails. Occasionally they would accept rides from farmers or other people kind enough to give them a ride.

The day was particularly warm and Molly sat on the tailgate of an old farm truck in a pile of straw, bouncing along a tiny dirt road, trying not to choke on the dust swirling under her feet. Pepper sat beside her, smoking a cigarette and looking like he didn't have a care in the world.

Actually, he looked like that most of the time, Molly thought to herself. What was his secret of confidence that he seemed to be overflowing with? And why did Molly already seem to have permanent worry lines in her face, even though she was only sixteen?

"You know what I think?" Pepper asked, breaking into Molly's solitary thoughts.

She turned to look at him. "What?"

"I'm really hungry for some roast chicken. It seems like we haven't had any real meat in ages." He inhaled again from the cigarette, making the end glow bright red, then extinguished it and flicked it away off the back of the truck.

"I think we should swipe one from a farmer who just seems to have too many."

The old truck bounced over a pothole in the road, jerking Molly from her position and forcing her to regain her balance.

"What!" she asked incredulously. "We're making more money now than we ever had before. Well, let me correct that statement.

We're *actually* making money now. We shouldn't be stealing things anymore."

He continued to stare off into the moving scenery in front of them. "I know. But I've been thinking that we might be getting a little tame lately. Being good all the time gets hard for me. I need a little more challenge. Something exciting. And I don't think those farmers will mind if just one chicken is gone."

Molly's eyes met Pepper's mischievous brown ones and she couldn't help but smile. "Tame?" she asked.

"Just think about the taste. Tender, delicious chickeny flavor! Much better than one we could get from the supermarket, even if we did have enough money to spend on one. And we won't get caught. I promise."

Later that night Molly found herself loping down a row of tall green stalks of corn behind Pepper. She couldn't believe that she was doing this. It seemed so old-school. But she trusted Pepper and followed close behind him until they came to a small farm. He stopped right behind where the corn field stopped.

There was a half moon out that night, just enough light shimmering to light their path but not so much as to clearly expose them. Grasshoppers sung so loudly in the grass around them that Molly thought that she could barely hear Pepper's heavy breathing beside her. They had left their things back at their camp by the river, and Molly enjoyed the feel of the rough cornstalks rubbing against her lower legs and bare feet.

"Now see that little building over there," Pepper pointed, his warm breath tickling her ear. "That's got to be the chicken coop. I'll just crawl in their little door and grab one by the legs. Chickens are heavy sleepers and the others won't notice a thing. You stay by the corner of the building and keep a lookout for anyone. I'll be in and out in a jiffy."

And with that, he sprang out from the cornfield and ran to the chicken coop, his bare feet making no audible noise on the slightly-wet grass. Molly followed close behind.

When he got there he immediately fell to his knees and crawled inside the coop. Molly stood outside, braced against the dark building, her heart pounding as she looked in the direction of the house. All of the lights in the building were off and she saw no movement within or around the little farmhouse. It seemed like forever before Pepper finally emerged from the chicken coop, hair full of feathers.

He held a limp bird in his hand with a smile brightening his face. He stood to his feet. "Too easy," he said, "almost makes me think that we should take another one—"

BANG! A spray of BB's blew a hole into the side of the chicken coop close to where Molly was standing. For a split second, Molly and Pepper looked at each other, eyes wide.

"Well, that makes it a little harder!" Pepper exclaimed a little too loudly, then whirled and ran as fast as his legs could carry him. Molly blasted off and was beside him in a second, focusing all of her attention on fleeing from the angry farmer.

"You no-good rotten thieves! Return that chicken to me immediately or I'll blow your heads off!" Molly heard him reload his shotgun and another blast aimed in their direction.

Pepper was breathing harder and harder as he ran, but what was making it even harder for him to breathe as he was laughing the entire time. "This is what I call fun," he said to Molly, laughing.

Molly doubled her strides and flew ahead of him along the cornfield trail they had made, back to the camp where their things were waiting. When she got there, Molly collapsed on the ground, exhausted. She felt as if her lungs were about to burst.

Pepper came along soon after. He sat on the ground beside her, breathing heavily. Molly looked at him, then at the chicken again. "You'd better plan on helping me clean and cook that thing," she said to him.

Pepper pulled out his pocket knife. "You bet I will."

Molly's stomach felt amazingly satisfied the next day. She had been afraid when they were caught in the act of thievery but had to admit that the tender, golden roasted chicken had tasted just as delicious as Pepper had described it to her.

The meat had seemed to give her a little more energy the next day as she traveled along with Pepper by her side. There was a bit of a spring in her step as she chatted with him. He was attempting to read a map that they had bought a few days ago, trying to determine where they were.

"We should be getting to another city fairly soon here," he said, staring intently at the map. Molly smiled to herself, hoping that he was right. Pepper hadn't told her much about his education, but Molly guessed that it was even less than she had.

"I like the cities," she said thoughtfully as they walked down the road, "we make more money there and there are more people to listen to us. But it does seem so very dirty in the city."

Pepper folded up the map and put it back into one of his pockets, listening to Molly talk.

"And it seems like people have much less morale there," she continued. "Everyone I see is so sad and depressed about the depression."

"Well," Pepper said, "that's why they call it a depression, because no one has a job and everyone's depressed."

Molly made a silly face at him. "That's not the reason."

"I think it is."

It was silent for a little while before Molly started talking again. "But the people in the small towns seem much more friendly and resourceful. We can always find a comfortable place to stay in the small towns."

As she said this she looked up to notice a dusty cloud up ahead in the distance. So there was a town not far ahead.

A few hours later, they were in the city. They walked along the side of the sidewalk, Pepper pointing out little landmarks, different kinds of shops and cars as they made their way through the city. Though the pair was cheerful, signs of the depression's effect on the people of that city were apparent everywhere. Almost one out of every three shops was out of business. There were a few hobos dressed in rags that Molly tried not to look at as she passed; sad excuses for what used to be men with families, jobs, and friends. It was one thing when the homeless vagabonds were just teens like Pepper and herself, out on the road for adventure and excitement. But it was quite another when it was men who were supposed to be supporting families.

A few men were selling fruit or trinkets on the street corners, trying to scratch out a little money. Molly's eyes were downcast as she passed by and tried not to gape. Pepper led Molly around a huge pile of household goods sitting on the sidewalk.

"Another reason I'm truly glad I'm homeless," Pepper said seriously as they passed. "I can't get evicted."

Molly didn't want to look but she couldn't help but stare at the huge pile of things that was stacked on the sidewalk. There were a couple dressers, a bed and mattress, clothing and other furniture. The family had apparently just gotten kicked out of their apartment and had nowhere to go. Her eyes strayed to a smaller object, a fuzzy brown teddy bear, and tears formed in Molly's eyes. To whom did the little teddy bear belong? A little girl, hungry and out on the street now probably with her mother and father, and brothers and sisters if she had them? Molly thought of the past when she was small and had a little toy of her own. Her mind wandered farther and farther away but she didn't let her tears fall as she followed behind Pepper down the city street.

Not long after, Pepper stopped and Molly nearly ran into him. "You hear that?" he asked. Molly stopped and calmed her swirling thoughts and tried to listen.

She looked at Pepper curiously. His eyes glimmered as he talked to her. "It's music. I don't think it's our kind of music really, but it's music nonetheless! Let's see if we can find out who's making it."

He started walking in the direction he thought the music was coming from, his long strides eating up the ground he had to cover in order to get there. Molly trotted behind him as he began to move a little faster along the street, determinedly following the sound.

He turned and walked across the street, went up the sidewalk a ways before turning to the left down an alley. Molly moved beside him, resolving not to let Pepper out of her sight in this big city. Newspapers blew along the alley and a shiver went down Molly's spine. What if they didn't want to meet these people anyway?

The music got louder and louder until they finally came to the place where the music was coming from. There was a small little kind of band playing, clanging out a song with instruments ranging from an old set of drums to tin cans to horns and trumpets.

The people obviously didn't belong to the same family but played together harmoniously nonetheless. There were about a dozen of them and all different skin colors were together and some were old and some were young, but Molly noticed that they were all male.

Pepper and Molly stood and watched the little band play their song. Molly watched curiously as a black man tapped out a rhythm on the drums, concentrating on the beat even when a drop of water slid down the building behind him and landed on one of his drums. A younger man played a horn, a curious sound Molly had never heard in her life but intrigued her.

She saw a young boy slapping tin cans on the ground, disrupting the flow of the music more than he helped out but no one seemed to pay too much attention to him as he irreverently banged out his own beat. But what really seemed to catch her eye was the boy they had on the guitar. He was about Pepper's age, rail thin like Pepper but not quite as tall, with pale blue eyes and blond hair. Somehow his eyes managed to meet Molly's and he winked at her.

Molly grinned and looked away to another member of the band until the song was over.

"What brings you folks out here? Doesn't look like you have much money to spare for the honor of watching our performance but you do look like you're carrying some instruments with you. Care to jam with us?" The man who had been playing the drums asked the two.

"I don't know, our music is kind of different from the kind that you play," Pepper said to him. "But do you know of any place that would let us perform for dinner and a place to stay for the night?"

The boy who had been playing the guitar set it aside and walked to where Molly and Pepper were standing. "I don't know if there's any place around here that would be open to that kind of arrangement," he stated as he walked around them in a circle, Pepper's eyes watching the entire time. "But you could play with us."

He put a hand on Molly's shoulder as he looked into her eyes and she felt as if her heart skipped a beat. "I don't think that I've heard your name yet."

"I'm Pepper," Pepper interrupted, "and she's Molly. Who are you?"

"Pepper? What kind of a name is that? Sounds like a kid nickname that someone never grew out of," the boy said, and Molly giggled subconsciously before she could stop herself. Pepper bristled and frowned darkly. The boy removed his hand from Molly's shoulder. "My name's Ronny."

His eyes moved to the instrument cases that both of them held. "What kind of instruments do you play anyway?" Ronny asked.

"Well," Molly started, "Pepper plays the guitar and I play the fiddle."

"The fiddle?" The tall dark man who had been playing the horn a few minutes ago was talking now. "I haven't heard one of those in ages! Pull it out, girl, and let's hear that fiddle sing!"

"We already have a guitar though so we won't be needing another one," Ronny said to Pepper, smirking.

"Nonsense!" the man said again, "we could use another rhythm guitar if he wants to play."

Molly was already rosining up her bow, grinning from ear to ear. "I don't know exactly how it will sound with all these other instruments," she told them, "and I don't know if we know any of the same songs, but I'll try my best."

Pepper was still frowning but had pulled out his guitar and had it ready sitting on his lap. Molly pulled her bow across the strings and the man behind her tapped out the starting signal on the drums.

"*One, two, one two three four!*" They started out in a song that Molly didn't know and she didn't join in right away but jumped in as soon as she could. Pepper sat behind her playing out the rhythm like he had known it all along.

Keep my skillet good and greasy
Gonna buy me a sack a flour
Bake a hoecake every hour
Keep my skillet good and greasy all the time, time, time

> *Honey if you say no,*
> *I'll never work no more*
> *I'll lay in your shanty all the time, time time,*
> *Keep my skillet good and greasy all the time, time time!*

Molly cracked a smile when she heard the silly lyrics. Her arm jerked back and forth as she adjusted to the rhythm of the music. Though she knew most of the men and boys around here had lived in the city for their entire lives, Molly could sense the country roots to a lot of the songs that they were playing. As she heard the lyrics sung, she made a mental note to memorize the song as best she could and add it to her repertoire.

> *Got some chickens in my sack*
> *Got the bloodhounds on my track*
> *Keep my skillet good and greasy all the time, time, time*

> *If they beat me to the door*
> *I'll sick 'em on the floor*
> *Keep my skillet good and greasy all the time, time, time!*

Molly moved out front and brought her violin higher, playing the notes out louder and louder as they got closer to the end of the song.

> *Gonna buy me a jug of brandy*
> *Gonna give it all to Nancy*
> *Keep her good and drunk and goosey all the time, time, time!*

When they were finished, most everyone broke out in laughter and quite a few of the men who had been playing put down their instruments and clapped and cheered for Molly. Molly smiled again, and bowed down with her fiddle at her side.

"You know," said Ronny, "if you guys don't have anywhere to stay tonight you could stay with us. We don't have a great place but we rent a little building on the outskirts of the city. We can get you a bunk to sleep in."

Molly blushed, embarrassed.

"No, we don't need a place to stay," Pepper said harshly, and began to put his guitar away. When he was finished, he turned to walk away. "But thanks anyway."

"But Pepper," Molly started, and Pepper stopped immediately at the sound of her voice and turned around, looking at her with an eyebrow raised.

"We don't have any place to stay tonight, and it's already after supper. We aren't going to be able to find any place to play, either," she said. Pepper gave her a strange look, and Molly wasn't sure that she could interpret it correctly, so she kept on. "I don't want to sleep on the streets."

Pepper sighed and put down his guitar case. "Alright," he said. "But we need to get an early start tomorrow."

Molly smiled, and turned to the members of the band. They were beginning to pack up their instruments and soon started walking down the street. Molly and Pepper followed close behind, until they came to a building as Ronny had said.

"Well, at least it's better than sleeping in the overcrowded homeless shelter downtown anyway," Ronny said when they got there. "Do you wanna join us for some supper around a fire before you settle down?"

The men had made a very small fire and warmed a small pot of stew over it. Molly sat beside Pepper with her hands on her knees, staring into the fire and contemplating the day's events. Molly sniffed the air, trying to determine what kind of stew was being made. It smelled like beans and tomatoes and she doubted if there was any meat in it. It was food, nonetheless. She was surprised at how kind these people were being to Pepper and herself. But she guessed that almost everyone who played great music was just a different kind of person, one who was hospitable and kind. It almost made her feel guilty, though, her and Pepper's savings of about five dollars that was sitting in her fiddle case could have been used to buy some food to share.

But then again, Pepper probably wouldn't have allowed her to waste it anyway. He sure seemed to be acting funny lately, Molly thought.

"Hey, Pepper," the horn player called out. "Do you want to bring your instruments inside and put them under your bunk?" Molly turned and handed her fiddle to Pepper, smiling. He didn't smile back as he grabbed the fiddle.

Molly sighed and put her head on her knees when Pepper went inside to put their things away. She saw a golden-haired boy walk up and sit right beside her close to the fire.

"Well, hello Ronny," she said. He smiled at her and began to talk with her.

Pepper's mouth nearly hung open when he walked back outside of the building to see Ronny sitting right beside Molly, gently grasping her hand and sweet talking her. He didn't say anything, but turned angrily and went right back inside.

That night, Molly lay beside Pepper on a small bottom bunk. She could hear the other men snoring and making other loud night noises as they drifted off into sleep. A sliver of moonlight poured into the room from a small window right into her face. She sunk her head into her pillow, trying to drown out the noises. Being unsuccessful, the turned around scooted a little closer to Pepper's large, warm body.

"Are you still awake, Pepper?" she asked softly, then looked at him.

"Yes," he said, staring up into the bottom of the top bunk, his arms crossed over his chest, with his brown eyes seeming unblinking and his tousled red hair sticking everywhere but flat on top of his head.

"This is kind of awkward, isn't it?" She asked. There had been only one empty bunk in the room and Pepper was the only person Molly trusted to share it with. "You finally got me in bed with you where you always wanted me," Molly joked.

Pepper only harrumphed and turned to face the opposite way. Molly felt more worried about him than she cared to admit. He was probably jealous about Ronny. But Pepper should know that she didn't really feel the same way about Ronny that Ronny obviously felt about her. And besides, it wasn't like Molly and Pepper were really a couple, anyway, and Pepper shouldn't be trying to control who she wanted to be with. Molly was her own person!

She laughed a little to herself. She had been telling herself that all along, ever since she had run away from home, and now she almost had to choose between two boys that had their eye on her! What had changed?

But, then again, Ronny was very handsome and he seemed really kind and paid attention to her. But Pepper had been very loyal throughout the months that they had been traveling together and he had never steered her wrong. She began to bite her fingernails subconsciously as she thought about her current situation. She would have to resolve the problems between Ronny and Pepper soon, because she couldn't stand it when Pepper acted this way.

Not long after midnight she finally pulled up the covers to her chin and fell asleep.

The next day when the sun was on the horizon, Pepper awoke and carefully made his way around Molly as he climbed out of the bed. His long lanky form cast a bit of a shadow over the bunk as he stood up, and he turned to look at Molly sleeping peacefully. He reached out with a tanned hand and tucked a stray piece of hair behind her ear.

There had been quite a few other girls in Pepper's life, ones that Molly knew nothing about. But Molly was different, she was special, and Pepper cared for her far more than he cared to admit.

And that is why he was determined to do this before she woke up. He went outside to stretch his legs a little, then came back inside, shutting the door silently behind himself.

He located the bunk where Ronny was sleeping, a top one, and shook him until he awoke. He looked confused as Pepper simply gestured for Ronny to follow him outside. Pepper walked outside confidently, not showing any apprehension in the least. His face turned dark as he scowled, thinking about Ronny.

The kid had to be a little older than himself, a man really, and Pepper despised his golden hair, small blue eyes and handsome features. He just knew that Ronny was a player, a heartbreaker for sure, and no matter how Molly felt about Ronny, Pepper had to keep him away from her.

"What's the big idea, waking me up before the sun's even all the way up and bringing me outside?" Ronny asked, still a little dazed from just being woke up.

Pepper turned and smiled at Ronny. "Well, we seem to be having a little problem."

Ronny seemed more alert now and scowled at Pepper. "What problem?"

"The problem with you stealing my girl."

"Stealing your girl? Ha! By the way she acted, I could hardly tell that you were more than her bus boy."

Pepper looked into Ronny's eyes and he spoke. "You are just scum that's probably already gone through dozens of naïve girls like her, ready to throw her away the minute another one comes along."

Ronny was taken aback a little. "I am not! But so what if I am? I could tell the girl would rather be with someone like me, anyway, someone who listens to her and seems to care about her, unlike the boy she drags along with her to play guitar backup."

Pepper felt a little hurt at Ronny's sharp words, but his temper flared and his hand slowly began to clench into a fist.

"And just give me awhile. I've got to be as good a guitar player as you are, probably better. She wouldn't mind having a handsome guy along with her to play guitar, and I could get Molly to dump you back alone on the streets in a second. That'd teach you a lesson about pride."

Pepper couldn't hold himself back any longer. He let his fist loose, slamming it into the side of Ronny's perfect face. "And I've got to teach you a lesson about stealing my girl."

Barely before he got it out, Ronny regained his composure and swung a fist at Pepper, but he ducked and Ronny went spinning around. Pepper shook his hand, trying to quickly relieve some of the burning pain before he threw another fist into Ronny. And another.

When Molly awoke, she stretched to her full length in the bed, noticing that Pepper was already up and gone from the bed. She got out of the bunk and went across to the door, just happening to meet Ronny in the doorway. She gave him a big smile. "How are you doing this morning?" she asked, but he didn't look at her.

"Fine," he answered tautly and moved past her and into the room.

Molly frowned a little to herself, wondering what was going on with Ronny. She shrugged it off and went outside, where she found Pepper talking to one of the band members.

"Hello, Molly," he said brightly. For how guarded Ronny had seemed, Pepper was quite cheerful. "Why don't you get your stuff together? I think we'd be best on our way. Milo says it's less than a hundred miles to New York city!"

Molly turned and walked back into the building. She met Ronny once again when she was inside, and this time she was able to see his face as he quickly glanced at her. She gasped quietly as he rushed past her. His face around his right eye was dark and swollen, and blood trickled down the corner of his mouth.

Molly scowled. She knew what had happened, and she knew the reason for the sudden mood swings of both the boys. She flew from the room, running back toward where Pepper stood outside.

"Molly!" he said, and smiled.

And before she could stop from her mad run Pepper moved to meet her and swept her up in his hands, kissing her softly on the lips. Molly fell limp in his strong arms, and lost her resolve to yell at Pepper till her face was purple, guilty as he was. She couldn't help but kiss him back, the sweetness of the kiss still somewhat foreign to her but so very delicious.

In the end it was Pepper who pulled away first. "You ready to go yet?"

She smiled at him, looking into his sparkling brown eyes and wondering why she had ever even considered dumping him for Ronny. And all she could do was nod dumbly at him, then turn around to get her things.

She had regained her composure as the two walked away from the city. It was obvious that Pepper really did care for her, but she still felt as if he had overreacted to Ronny.

"You didn't have to do that, you know," she said to him as they walked down the road.

Pepper turned and looked at her, a little surprised, but kept walking as he spoke. "Do what?"

"Don't act dumb, Pepper," Molly said, annoyed. "I know you beat up Ronny." The burning flame of anger that had started in her died down a little, but the embers were still there and she wanted to let Pepper know.

"Well, he deserved it."

"I don't know if he deserved it, Pepper."

"Well, I think he did if he was trying to steal my girl."

Silence.

"Who says I'm your girl anyway?" Molly asked him, irritated.

"Your lips do," Pepper answered with a smirk.

Molly opened her mouth but couldn't come up with a reply.

"I guess you and I both know that we're more than musical partners now, and if you feel that's wrong I can leave our little group."

"I don't think it's wrong if I do a little flirting with another boy," Molly said.

"Aw, shucks Molly, you knew that boy was a player and was only out to get one thing."

Molly didn't know why, but she still seemed to feel angry toward Pepper, even though he hadn't done a lot of wrong.

Pepper moved his bulky guitar case to his left hand then slowed down a little so that Molly walked right beside him, and held out his hand. "That Ronny was a wimp anyway. Ran away before I could even finish teaching him his lesson."

Molly smiled, looking into Pepper's eyes, then finally began to laugh hysterically. She grabbed his hand and began to stroll along at a skipping gait, dragging Pepper along with her as they traveled closer and closer to their destination.

Molly and Pepper traveled farther and farther east, playing at stops all along the way. They made enough money to keep themselves fed and a little extra, and Molly always stuffed it into the little compartment inside her violin case.

For the first time in a long while, Molly seemed happy. Her grandfather's old fiddle was serving her well; very well, and her nomadic lifestyle satisfied her craving for freedom out on the open road. That little circle of space that was her past seemed nonexistent, and that seemed to be all she required to be happy. She almost didn't care if they did get to New York, she felt as if she would be content traveling as a musician for the rest of her days. Pepper had changed throughout their journeys, and Molly knew that he was no longer a stranger but a good friend that she could depend on for companionship and even protection.

She was meeting more people than she ever would have imagined, learning more things, discovering new songs, music types and instruments.

She sat by their campfire one night, scribbling on a little notebook that they had bought in the last town. "It's amazing how many new songs I've learned," Molly said to Pepper as she scribbled. Pepper threw a few more pieces of wood into the fire and then came over to sit next to her.

Molly struggled to see by the light of the setting sun on the horizon and the bit of flickering fire that Pepper had built. "You know," she said, "I might even try to write some of my own songs."

"That would be interesting," Pepper thought out loud.

It was silent except for the scratching of Molly's pencil on her paper until the sun had finally sunk so low that Molly couldn't see anymore.

Pepper sighed, looking into the fire. "Molly," he said quietly, "what ever happened to your family?"

Molly abruptly turned to look at him intently.

"I mean, I know you ran away and all that, but was it really so terrible that you had to run away? Or did you just want some freedom? Or what?"

Molly poked at the fire with a stick, wondering whether she should answer his question or not.

"You don't have to tell me," Pepper said. "I know you seem to be a little sore about it, but I am just curious."

"Well," Molly began, "my father was a farmer out in Nebraska. Times were pretty good when I was little, we grew tons of wheat and had all kinds of animals. Milk cows, horses, chickens, pigs, and beef cattle. He borrowed money from the bank to expand, and we had more than three hundred acres of land. Then the dust came."

The fire crackled loudly and Molly paused for a moment.

"The neighbors all said it was topsoil that came from Kansas; that big rolling cloud of black dust. It blew over our fields and choked our animals, blew in all the cracks of our house and covered all of our belongings with dirt. Everywhere there was dirt. Me and my two younger brothers did the best we could to help out our ma and pa, running outside nearly every hour to wipe down the cattle's noses with a wet cloth, to shut in the chickens, to sweep the dirt out of the house and shake it from the clothes."

She stopped again, thinking about her past.

"My pa used to beat me. Oh, I hated it, but once the dust came he seemed to stop a little; I think he was so mad that he couldn't bring himself to take it out on me. He just sat with his head in his hands, crying even sometimes, and I felt like I could withstand the beatings if only he would be happy again.

"But just as quickly as the dust had come, it was gone, taking the precious Nebraska growing soil with it. There had been a terrible drought the last year, and it didn't help our situation at all. Most of our neighbors had already moved to the cities. The banks called in their loans as the depression hit us the hardest, and we didn't eat well but my father was determined to stay and paid most of the loans back. I always had loved our farm horses but those were the first things we sold. I couldn't stand watching cows, pigs and chickens die every day. My ma became a fatigued, short-tempered bag of bones and my father did too. Their frustrations were poured out heavy on me, and only because I was the oldest. But both of my brothers and I were starving, and we all knew it.

"I don't think my pa cared much though. He was too stubborn about the land. He refused to let us try to find outside work and he didn't seek it out himself, either. I didn't know what to do, the tension between me and my parents seemed to be too much, and I knew that I was just another mouth to feed.

"So, I took off, bringing my grandfather's old fiddle with me. Before he died, he showed me all he knew and since then all I could do was perfect his techniques. I was determined to make my way in the world, job or no job. I didn't have any relatives to stay with, so I didn't try to find any place to stay.

"Sure, it was hard at first. It seemed like no one cared to hear good fiddle music, much less pay for it. Through hard work, dedication and the kindness of a lot of people, though, I somehow perfected my little 'act' and figured out how to survive out on the road.

"I don't think that I always wanted to go to New York City, but it was always kind of in the back of my mind. I don't think that it will be any brighter there in terms of the depression, but there's sure to be some opportunities waiting for us there."

Pepper nodded, thinking about all that Molly had just poured out to him. He was glad that she trusted him enough to tell him all about her past, but all the information she had given him was still swirling around his head. All he had known her as was a traveling musician, a girl who did mostly whatever she pleased and went wherever she wanted, answering to no one. He had no idea that she had such a family.

"There's got to be," he said. They both didn't want to face the reality of what would happen if they couldn't find a steady gig in New York.

"What will we do if there is nothing for us there?" Molly finally asked. "Will we just have to turn around and head back to where we came from? Attempt to settle down and start a family?"

Molly sensed Pepper jump a little when she said that, but Molly continued, "Because there's no way I can go back to my own family. I obviously don't belong there."

"Don't worry about it," Pepper said cheerfully and put his hand around her shoulders. "If it really is hopeless in New York, we'll just turn around and head all the way back to Californ-ee. They say there's jobs there, and of course there's thousands of miles from New York to California so we'd probably have the rest of our life to explore the nation. Even then, if we wanted to get there sooner I bet I could find a way to ride the rails all the way there in less than a week!"

Molly laughed. "Well, I'm glad you have a backup plan, anyway."

Pepper grinned, his face illuminated by the small campfire. Molly always found his smile so contagious and smiled back as she looked into his eyes. And for the first time ever, Molly felt as if she was truly happy. Almost as if she had found her place in the world.

Chapter 9

Molly and Pepper traveled further and further eastward, playing in a different place almost every night, hopping trains and dodging cops. The summer months flew by in a breeze, going much too fast for Molly and Pepper. Soon the leaves began to fall, but not their hopes.

Footsore and weary, but not the least bit discouraged, they stood a couple miles outside the great New York City. Smog drifted from the smokestacks from within the heart of the city, buildings rose up high into the sky, and the air even smelled different. Molly stopped and stared into the city ahead; the great unknown. Pepper stopped walking and turned to look back at her. "What's wrong Molly?"

"We're finally there."

"Don't worry about it, Molly. We'll be fine. We'll have a whole new life inside that city."

Molly instinctively pulled her violin closer to her, her blue-green eyes still staring ahead. "But what if it's not what we expect?" her lips hardly moved as she spoke quietly.

Knowingly, Pepper smiled at her. "Of course it won't be what we expect. But it could be even better. Let's just take life as it comes, okay?" He reached out his hand to her, and she moved forward to take hold of it. Together they kept walking into the abyss of New York City.

New York City was even busier than they expected. Cars flew back and forth, newsboys called out the headlines, men on street corners everywhere sold nearly everything from apples to jewelry. Garbage was all over the streets, tucked into every place imaginable and collecting in the gutters.

A small boy shouldered Molly roughly as they walked but he didn't bother to say he was sorry. People crowded the sidewalks, squeezing past each other to reach their destinations more quickly. All the bustle made Molly's head spin.

Pepper grabbed her arm and pulled her close as they walked, attempting to guard her. "We should try to find a place to play," he said to her.

She only nodded and looked around at the variety of buildings surrounding them. Where would they start? She noticed a tall building that had people flowing in and out of it. PUBLIC LIBRARY the sign above read. "Can we go in there?" She asked Pepper.

Pepper stopped and looked to where she was pointing. "Sure, I guess."

Molly pulled him up the marble stairs and into the building. Her mouth dropped open as she walked in. Books were lined up in shelves everywhere! A few librarians sat at the main desk in the center, sorting through card catalogs and helping patrons find and check out books.

Casually Pepper strolled in behind Molly as they entered the building, looking around himself with a little interest. Molly let her hand drag across the spines of the books as she walked, relishing the feeling of so much knowledge in her hands, and soon cracked one open that she found interesting. She read the first few paragraphs, then made her way to a comfy chair and sat down, still reading the type the whole way there.

It took her a while to realize that Pepper was still standing beside her with his guitar case on the ground beside him and hands in his pockets. She looked up quickly. "Go ahead, Pepper, grab a book. You can read too, I think we can take some time off to enjoy ourselves a little."

He didn't meet her eyes as he said quietly, "I can't read."

Molly tried not to act too surprised and thought before she opened her mouth again to speak, but Pepper spoke first.

"You can stay here and read what you like. I'll go look to see if we can find a place to play for the night. Just promise not to get into trouble while I'm gone, and *stay here.*"

Molly was finally able to meet his gaze. "I promise."

Pepper exited the library and Molly delved into the book, amazed at the world it was taking her to. At first her thoughts bothered her and she continued to think about Pepper. How hard it would be not being able to read! He was missing out on a whole different world. She made up her mind to teach him, if she could find the time and if she had the skill to do it. But the story overwhelmed the thoughts tucked in the back of her mind, and it felt like only a few moments before Pepper stood in front of her again, ready to go.

Reluctantly she placed the book back onto the shelf, she had only gotten about halfway through it but she planned to finish it as soon as she could. "So did you find any place for us to play?" she asked Pepper.

"I've looked for hours," he said, "but I couldn't find a good place for us to play. There's just too much competition in the area."

"Oh," Molly said, her countenance downcast.

"But I did find one place for us to play, but the only thing they've got to offer us is a place to stay."

Molly smiled reassuringly. "We've got to start small," she said, "before we can think big."

The pair played in a café that night, and continued to play at a different place every night. Molly had fun, but still seemed to worry about whether or not they would find a permanent gig in New York City. *But could it be . . .no,* she thought *there's no way all these people could be showing up just for us.* But it did seem that as more and more people heard about Molly and Pepper, the bigger their audiences got. But they hadn't even put up any kind of a flyer or anything, and Molly didn't think that word of mouth could travel that far and fast.

But Pepper seemed convinced. "The longer we stay around," he told her, "the more people will have a chance to hear about us, and we'll get more and more popular."

Molly and Pepper had had plenty of time to perfect their act, adding jokes and stories and even little musical tricks that made the crowd go crazy.

During the day Molly and Pepper spent their time searching for places to play in the nearly endless expanse of what was New York City, dodged street smart scammers and explored the different shops and public buildings.

One day as they walked past a particular part of the city, Pepper stopped.

"See that over there," he said, pointing. Molly turned her gaze and noticed a large stage with people crowded all around it. A political speaker was there, ranting about one of the latest laws passed, waving his arms around and speaking with such utter authority and direction that his audience was spellbound.

"We could use that to perform. I think it belongs to the city, but I'm not sure. If we could get up there after someone speaks to a huge crowd, just think about all the people we could play for! Let's go over there and take a look."

The pair pushed their way through the crowd of people then stopped when they got near the front, trying to listen in on what the man was saying. It seemed, however, that they had gotten there too late, as the man thanked the crowd for their time and climbed off the stage shortly after they had arrived. Molly was disappointed, she had really wanted to hear what the man had to say but she didn't have time to think about it because Pepper was pulling on her sleeve.

"Come on, now's our chance!" he said, "let's get up there." Molly shook her head but Pepper was already dragging her up the stairs of the stage. She wasn't ready for it, but there she was, standing on the stage with hundreds of people watching her. Her knees shook and her mouth felt dry and cottony. What was Pepper thinking? She had performed tons of times before but really she was just a farm girl at heart, and that was all she thought she would ever really be.

"Don't just stand there, pull out your fiddle!"

Pepper was already playing a chord progression, waiting for Molly to start. Molly expected the people to all disperse since the man was finished talking, some of them did but most of them stayed, their eyes intent on her. Nervously, she grasped the neck of her fiddle and brought it out from its case.

She was so nervous she barely thought about what to play but her hands automatically began to play a familiar tune. She started out on one string but soon was sawing away on both and making her way from one end of the stage to the other.

Molly took the violin from under her chin and put it by her side, shakily beginning to sing the first verse,

Went up on the mountain top
Just to give my horn a blow,
Thought I heard my true love say
"Yonder comes my beau!"

Before she knew it the once-silent crowd began to clap to the beat, and Molly's face lit up with a smile as she swirled her skirt and danced, singing out the chorus.

Bile them cabbage down, down, turn them hoecakes round.
The only song that I can sing is bile dem cabbage down!

The tap, tap, tap of her feet matched the clapping of the crowd, which had become so loud that her single violin could hardly be heard over the noise. She picked up her skirt and swirled it around, danced from one end of the stage to the other, then, feeling cocky, stopped to give Pepper a quick peck on the cheek.

His face turned cherry red but he continued to play the chords for her. Molly brought her violin back up to her neck and played the notes of the old familiar tune, faster and faster she played, getting caught up in the enthusiasm of the crowd.

Once again the fiddle was at her side; she felt euphoria bubbling up inside of her and she raised her hand to the crowd. Sunlight filtered down on her through the city, her long shadow cast behind her on the stage. Her voice started out loud in the chorus of the song, until the people down below her began to sing as well and drowned out her tiny single voice.

The crowd was made up of people from all walks of life. There were children and adults, old people and even some babies in the crowd. There were some of the few rich but mostly poor city folk who had no jobs, clothing complete with tears and holes. But nearly all of them were smiling; Molly had made their day better and the thought made her heart sing.

Her enthusiasm, however, was put off for a minute when she noticed a tall man standing down in the crowd wearing a dark coat and a derby hat. He was not smiling, but looked as if he was pondering the pair playing in front of him on the stage. He had dark hair, eyes, and a moustache at which he scratched at continuously. Molly was almost thrown off by the strange look on his face, but continued to play, though she still snatched a glimpse of his face every now and then.

Finally she sharply pulled the bow across the strings on the last note, ending the song with a look of triumph on her face.

The crowd roared, throwing Molly off only a little. She knew that people usually enjoyed their music, but she wasn't expecting anything like this.

"Get her a microphone!" she heard someone call out, and one was hastily set up in front of her.

The people below her were quiet now. She tucked a piece of hair behind her ear, then self-consciously smoothed out the wrinkles in her skirt. Nervously she cleared her throat.

"Hello there," she started, "uh, my name is Molly. Molly Johnson. This here's Pepper, the fastest guitar player this side of the Mississippi. We've both been traveling across the nation, discovering new songs, techniques and meeting new people. We'd both like to--"

She was cut short when she felt someone tapping on her shoulder. She turned to see a man wearing-official looking clothes staring down his nose at her, then turned her gaze to see Pepper watching them with a apprehensive look on his face.

"Yes?" she asked quietly.

"Do you have a permit to be performing in this area?" he asked her.

"Um, I, uh, wait—" Molly stuttered.

"Maybe you should come with me," the man said, taking her arm gently and leading her off the stage. She didn't want to leave but her feet felt compelled to follow him. Out of the corner of her eye she noticed Pepper standing up from his chair.

Molly heard the crowd boo loudly and a chair flew violently onto the stage. Agitatedly Molly began to chew her fingernails on her hand, worried about what was going to happen to her.

Suddenly the man behind her was pulled to a halt and Molly stopped along with him. She turned to see Pepper firmly gripping the man's arm. "Where do you think you're taking her?" he asked sternly.

"I'm just going to take her down to the station and we'll get this figured out and see if we need to give her a citation."

"You shouldn't do that."

"Well I should take you, too, freckle-face," the man said and twisted out of Pepper's grip to get a hold on his skinny arm.

WHACK!

Molly heard it before she saw it, but even then she felt a sickening feeling in her gut. Pepper had punched the man square in the jaw and didn't have time to reach for Molly before he returned the blow. Hunched over, Pepper held his now-bleeding nose for a second before standing up again.

Molly couldn't believe she was doing it, but before she knew it she came up from behind the man and beat on his back, giving Pepper a moment to regain his composure.

Only a few seconds later all hell broke loose. Tensions were already tight because of the harsh times, and the event seemed to push the people over the edge. They were already looking for a reason to create a disturbance, but the definite break in opinions threw the crowd into chaos. Some of the men from the crowd climbed up onto the stage and began to beat on the officer, but reinforcements were already there, attempting to tame the wild crowd. The man who had originally attempted to lead Molly off the stage was long gone and Molly stood smack dab in the middle of the confusion, watching the mess of people swirl around her.

People shoved Molly from the left and the right and she stood on tiptoes to try to see where Pepper was in the dozens of people that were not fighting. She finally gave up, infuriated with the stupidity of the people around her and opened her fiddle case again, taking out her bow. If she couldn't get them to stop civilly, she might as well join the fight. What was one more person in this huge mess? A mad ball of fury, she brandished her new-found weapon on any man she saw wearing any type of uniform.

She slapped it hard across one man's ear, making him wince in pain. "Aha!" she laughed gleefully, but the smile was suddenly wiped off Molly's face when she saw the man turn angrily to her. Jumping backward slightly, she waved her bow menacingly at him. He showed no fear at all but advanced toward her. Stifling a little scream, she turned around to run, but her nose ran right into the man behind her.

Molly stuttered for a second, but before she could turn to run away she felt someone grab her again, yanking her backwards into him. She twisted to get away but Pepper held onto her tighter.

"Come on, let's get out of here!" he told her. Together, they ran from the crowd, fleeing the scene of mob confusion. Molly could almost see their escape route; where they would be able to get away without being noticed but she followed wherever Pepper would lead her.

But once again Molly felt Pepper get yanked away from her, and she turned to see a burly man holding on to Pepper with an iron-like grip. Mumbling a curse word under her breath, she took her bow that had been still at her side and brought it down on the man, but with his free arm he grabbed the bow and snapped it like a twig. Molly's mouth gapped open with astonishment for a moment, then the anger boiled up inside her and she rushed at the man.

A sudden blow from behind brought Molly to her knees.

"That girl has no sense. No sense whatsoever. Common street trash." She heard a man talking behind her, but her vision clouded and the objects that she saw began to swirl around.

"Molly? Molly!"

The last thing she noticed was mixture of worry and anger written on Pepper's face before she felt herself go faint in his arms.

Chapter 10

Molly awoke with a fierce pounding in her head. She sat up and put her hand to her head, looking around herself.

"My fiddle!" she cried loudly, then stood to her feet. "Where is my fiddle?"

"Calm down, girl." A rough-looking woman with her back against the wall spoke to her.

"A cell?" Molly asked anxiously, her head throbbing harder than ever. "Pepper? Where did Pepper go?"

She looked around the dark room and felt the hot tears beginning to squeeze out from the corners of her eyelids. She couldn't believe that she had ended up in jail. In jail! Had they really came this far just to end up in prison?

Molly took a second to look around herself. The cell was dark, with only a few small windows up on either side of the room, and the dank smell made her want to gag. There were about four other women that shared the cell with her, all fairly dirty with unpleasant looks on their faces, except for the woman who had talked to her. She seemed to be at least a little kind, so as Molly leaned her head against the bars she spoke again. "I don't even remember why I'm here," she said miserably. She looked nervously at the other women who were around her, swallowed and turned to look back at the woman who had spoken to her.

The woman twisted her hands around to make a little knot in some kind of fabric she held in her hand, and without looking up she answered. "You were hosting a performance without a permit, or some such nonsense like that. I don't know why they locked you up, you sure don't look like a public nuisance to me." She had looked up from her work now and was squinting hard at Molly, critically examining Molly's thin, youthful frame.

Molly pulled her nose from between the bars and turned to look at the woman again. It all flooded back to her then, she remembered what a mess they had made the day before. The woman still sat crouched with her back up against the wall, her thin dirty hair falling into her face as she worked on her project with dark bony hands.

"And yer sweetheart ain't here, either. They've got him locked up in the men's quarters. I'm not sure where they've got that instrument of yours, but I think it has probably been confiscated and is locked up in the main office."

Molly just blinked again, still looking at the woman.

"So what might your name be?" she asked.

"Mo-Molly," she stuttered.

She was surprised to notice that the other three cell mates said or did nothing, a couple of them staring Molly down and one other one staring into the distance with a glazed look over her face.

"Well, my name's Majorie. If you're wondering, too, I'm in here for stealing is all. Sometimes you wonder why they even bother locking us up anyway, so many of us got to do it. But you'll like it here, anyway. They feed ya, and give you a place to stay," she said with a laugh. "It's better than most can claim out there on the streets."

"No!" Molly said. "I mean, I want to be free."

The woman just laughed and continued working. Molly sat down and sulked.

"I wonder how much the fine is that I'm supposed to pay," she said quietly.

"You'll never be able to pay it anyway. They're usually pretty stiff," Majorie said. "I think yours would probably be around $15."

Molly cringed when she heard Majorie say that. She knew that the most she and Pepper had at the time couldn't have been much more than seven or eight dollars.

Molly's head fell in her hands and she began to sob quietly, until she finally drifted off into a restless sleep.

Molly didn't know how long she would be in the prison, or how much her fine was, or even where Pepper was at. They were given food twice a day, but the crabby old woman who served it to them was impervious to Molly's questions. Molly cried herself to sleep two nights in a row in the dark cell bunk, but quietly tried to keep it to herself for fear of bothering her rather irritable cell mates. She couldn't imagine how long she would be kept inside the dark prison walls. Would it be forever?

And I don't even have my fiddle to break the monotony of this cell life, Molly thought to herself three days later as she sat in her cell. Actually, any activity at all would be preferable to this kind of slow, lazy torture, but her fingers itched to play her fiddle. The women said that they would be taken out to do community service occasionally, but Molly doubted if it would ever happen. She could see through the smudged windows that the days were getting shorter and it wasn't much longer before the snow would begin to fall. The thought depressed Molly even more, and silent tears ran down her face as she stared into the corner of the room.

"Excuse me miss," Molly jumped when she heard a man speaking to her. She turned to look outside of her cell, and noticed a police officer standing outside along with another serious-looking man.

"Molly—right?" the man beside the officer asked quietly.

Molly's eyes were open wide gazing at him, she could hardly form her lips into an appropriate answer so she just nodded.

"Why don't you come with us, then?" The officer said. "This man wants to speak with you."

The cell door was opened and Molly walked out of the dark cage-like prison for the first time in three days, wondering what was going to happen to her next.

She followed the two men out of the room and down a small hallway until they came to a room that looked like an office. Suddenly Molly's violin case was handed to her, and she took a look at it for a second before snatching it instinctively.

The man motioned for her to sit down on one end of a desk, and the officer left and the other tall man sat down in the chair on the other side of the desk.

Molly couldn't help herself, she didn't pay any attention to the man in front of her but opened her violin case on her lap, pulling out its contents and smoothing her hand over the beautiful finish of her old fiddle. She opened the little compartment and found all of her belongings still safely stashed inside. Lastly she took out her bow, and the smile on her face fell as the bow fell limp in the middle.

The whole time Molly looked over her belongings the man watched in silence, twisting his little bit of a moustache carefully. His dark hair was trimmed neatly and not one piece of it fell into his serious brown eyes. He was waiting for the perfect moment, and Molly had just afforded it to him that minute.

He carefully pulled out a brand new violin bow from under the desk and gently handed it to Molly. Molly looked up from the disappointing bow she held in her hand and saw the man offering her the new bow.

Graciously she took it from him, then looked up at him.

His lips moved in a weird way as he began to talk, making his face seem thoughtful before he spoke.

"Molly," he addressed her, "I heard you and Pepper play in town a few days ago."

He paused for a minute, carefully choosing his words. Molly just continued to look at him with wide eyes, gently gliding her hands across the top of the bow as he spoke and wondering how the man knew their names.

"I believe you two are good. Really good. And the last place you belong in is prison."

Molly stopped and looked at the man even more intently, her green eyes holding his gaze. The tension in the room felt like a string about to snap under the pressure, and Molly wondered if she was dreaming.

"I think that you could have your own show," he continued, "a radio show. Nothing much, really just a half hour every Thursday night or something like that."

Molly could hardly believe what she was hearing. Was this right? Was a complete stranger really offering her a gig? And even one on the radio? She was nearly speechless.

"You both—Pepper especially—really have a character developed. You two would make darned good radio personalities, not to mention how much people would love your music.

"I'm paying your fine--$15--so that you can get out of here and I'll give you a place to stay. I can't promise that the pay will be good right away, but publicity will soar for you two, and where there's publicity, there's always money," he said with a smile.

Molly still couldn't say anything, she still just nodded stupidly at the man. She closed her violin case and looked up.

Leading Pepper into the room, another officer entered and then gestured for Pepper to take a seat beside Molly. Molly's eyes lit up and a smile instantly flashed across her face. Pepper sat down beside her and she opened her mouth to talk but before she could Pepper pursed his lips and leaned over the arm of the chair towards Molly.

"Wait there!" the man said suddenly, and Molly and Pepper paused and their eyes averted to the right to look at him, both still leaning to reach each other in an embrace. "None of that stuff! You two are supposed to talk about this together, and decide if it is an option you want to consider."

Pepper frowned. "Consider?" he asked irritably. "It's a done deal already, mister." And with that he tenderly kissed Molly right in front of the man, not bothering to take much notice of the man until he stood up with an exasperated sigh and left.

Molly skipped ahead of Pepper and the man, gleefully pointing out the tall buildings and other unique parts of the landscape to where they were traveling. She could hardly believe that this was happening. It made her so excited, but she felt nervous down in the pit of her stomach at the same time.

The man had driven them to a cleaner part of town and they got out of the car and were walking up to the building where Molly and Pepper were to stay. They entered the building through glass doors and came to the main office where the man spoke with the secretary, then escorted them to an elevator where they went up so many floors so fast that it made Molly's head spin.

Straightening his jacket, the man exited the elevator with the pair following. "Here is your room," he said to them, gesturing to allow Pepper to open the door.

Pepper took the opportunity and pushed the door open, gaping as he went in.

"Wow!" Molly said under her breath as they entered. It was a complete apartment, with a couple bedrooms, a dining room, kitchen and living area.

Pepper looked skeptically at his surroundings, then set his guitar case down and ran his fingers through his long rust-colored hair. He then brought his hand to the side of his head, contemplating. But Molly knew that he was pleased, no matter how cool he tried to act.

The man smiled smugly to himself, enjoying the scene that the two street ragamuffins were making in the beautifully furbished apartment. And this was only the lower-class stuff! He couldn't imagine what their response would be if they became popular enough to enjoy the really good life. He didn't let them on though and pulled a watch out of his pocket pretending to look at the time with a bored expression on his face.

"So how do you like it?" he asked them quietly.

"We love it!" said Molly enthusiastically, beaming with joy.

"There is another apartment on this floor for Molly," he said, "unless you two will be sharing one."

Molly shook her head, and the man continued. "I'll be acting as your agent from now on. I'm not sure of your complete schedule but we'll start out with tomorrow evening when we record your first broadcasting. Oh, and there is one more surprise for you on the dining room table."

Pepper had already lost his cool and was rushing for the table, where he found two familiarly shaped cases, brand new. Pepper was already prying open the larger one. Molly looked to the smaller one, and she could guess what it was.

"Oh shucks, look at this guitar! It's gleaming; brand new!" Pepper nearly hollered with excitement when he opened the case. He pulled out the guitar and strummed it, producing the most amazingly clear and smooth musical notes that Molly had ever heard from a guitar.

The man watched Molly expectantly. She set her old fiddle case down and opened the smaller one that was on the table. Inside was a beautiful violin, crafted with excellence and polished until it shone. Molly picked it up and looked at it, then turned it around with unbelief. Calmly she set it back down into the case.

"I'm sorry. It's beautiful, but I can't use that instrument," Molly said.

Disappointment showed through on the man's face. "Why not?" he asked.

"I don't really know," said Molly, "I've been using this fiddle of my grandfather's for almost seven years now. It may be old, but it has gone with me everywhere and I think it should come with me here too. I'm sure it has sufficient tone quality and volume for whatever you'll have me do with it."

Pepper had stopped messing with his new guitar, and it was quiet for awhile before Molly began to speak again. "I guess it has just become a part of me now. I can't use a different one."

The man smiled now. "That's okay," he said. "It shouldn't be a problem." He scooped up the violin case in his arms and began to make his way out of the door. "Oh," he added, "if you need room service dial seven on the telephone. And remember, tomorrow evening at six o'clock! Have a nice night!"

Then he left the room, shutting the door behind him.

Pepper and Molly looked at each other simultaneously. "Oh my gosh!!" Molly yelled, but Pepper had already turned in a dead run then jumped into the air, landing square on the bed in a giant belly flop.

Molly followed after him gleefully and then sat on the bed beside him, straightening her skirt over her legs. Pepper rolled over on his belly and rested his head on one hand, grinning one of the silliest grins Molly had ever seen him wear, with his red hair falling into his freckled face, flopped over one of his brown eyes.

When he smiled like that, however, Molly found it irresistible and smiled right back at him. "I can't believe that this is really happening," she said to him.

"Me either!" he replied enthusiastically. "I just hope it lasts."

"Hope it lasts?" Molly repeated, confused.

"Yeah, that man seems real nice, but you know he's only out there for one thing—our money."

"Aw, it doesn't matter," Molly said, "we never make any money anyway. Well, just enough to live by, anyhow. And look at this nice place! And he even paid our fine so we could get out of prison sooner."

Pepper shuddered. "At least we're not in there anymore." Then he smiled. "And we're together now."

At six o'clock sharp the next evening, Molly and Pepper stood together inside a small studio. Pepper held his guitar poised and ready to go, Molly held her violin's neck and her bow scrunched together in one hand, a script in the other , a worried look on her face.

"I don't know how we're going to do this, Mr. Peterson," Molly said to the man who had helped them thus far. "Pepper can't even read."

From behind her back Pepper made a face at her, but Mr. Peterson smiled confidently. "It'll be alright. Just act natural. You'll do most of the reading anyway."

Molly continued to hold her violin at her side and peered at what they called "the can" curiously. She was supposed to talk inside of that. Mr. Peterson went behind the soundboard with three other men and signified that she was to begin. Molly cleared her throat nervously and began.

"Hi-my-name-is-Molly-and-this-is--"

"STOP! Stop! Hold on there."

Molly heard a buzzing sound and the men looked disappointedly at her. "That's no way to read a script! You sound terrible! Do you even know how to read aloud? Let's try it again."

Molly started again, but with the same consequence. Mr. Peterson shook his head, wondering if it was really worth it at all. With the rage of words that followed, Pepper noticed the hurt look on Molly's face and brazenly took matters into his own hands.

"Alright, alright, let me show you how we usually get things done around here," he said, gently pushing Molly away and walking up to the can. "It's rather impromptu. Signal me when we're ready to go."

The men behind the soundboard just looked at each other, confused, until one of them shrugged and flipped a switch. He then gave Pepper the signal.

"Hello there, New York, and welcome to our new show! My name is Pepper, it's always been Pepper, nothing more, nothing less, and my partner Molly. Say hello, Molly."

"Hello." Molly tried to make her voice sound stronger than it actually was.

"I play the guitar," Pepper spoke into the can, "and Molly plays fiddle. The best darn fiddle you'll ever hear this side of the Mississippi!"

Molly blushed, but didn't think about the fact that it didn't matter because the audience couldn't see her face anyway.

"What's that Molly? You blushin'?"

When he said that her cheeks turned an even more crimson color but she noticed that the men were smiling now. Apparently they liked Pepper's casual tone.

"The first song we're gonna play is called 'Blackberry Blossom' and it's a favorite around our part of the country, we hope that you like it."

He then pulled his guitar strap around his shoulders and played out the chord sequence, leaving it up to Molly to play out the melody.

The song sounded a bit hollow to Molly in the artificial environment that she wasn't used to, but she did have to admit that Pepper's new guitar sounded beautiful and added a lot to their little duet. She switched things up a bit and played a couple of double stops on her violin strings while Pepper took his turn playing the melody. She grinned secretly to herself when she saw the people in the room smile hugely at them, obviously surprised at how good the two kids actually were.

When the song was over Pepper walked over to the can again and began tell a joke, his eyes glancing up toward the clock.

"Times are getting desperate, pretty hard, but there still is a little humor in a lot of the things I see on a daily basis." Pepper laughed. "As I walked past a car dealership only a few days ago I heard a man speaking to the salesman. 'Forget all the fancy sales talk!' he says, 'How much gas is there in the tank?'"

Pepper bellered out a laugh and Molly giggled with him.

"Molly knows one, too," he said when he was finished, then gestured for her to come over by him. "It's about that favorite president of yours, Mr. Hoover, though I believe I might have been told not to use political jokes on this show . . ." he trailed off, leaving the can to Molly.

Molly put her mouth in front of it timidly and cleared her throat. She managed to get the whole joke completed without stuttering too much, and by the end of it she seemed to actually be enjoying herself.

They played a few more songs and told a few more jokes and funny stories before their twenty-five minutes were up and they made up a conclusion to their act.

The men behind the soundboard clicked a few switches, took off their headphones and came over to the pair. "You two are great," one of them was saying, shaking Pepper's hand. "If the audience doesn't like that, I don't know what they will!"

"Well, thank you," Pepper was saying, Molly just sat back a little and watched the small commotion.

"I'm so glad you found these two, Mr. Peterson. They are fresh and new, something that the people of New York are really wanting now. But I guess all that we can do right now is put it on the air and see what happens." The rest of the men smiled at them and shook Molly's and Pepper's hands, thanking them before they left.

Molly and Pepper's show—Molly with a Dash of Pepper—soared to the top of the popularity charts in radio. Though not nearly as famous as other comedy shows such as "Amos n' Andy", Molly and Pepper's lighthearted show appealed to audiences of all ages.

It wasn't exactly an "overnight deal", as Pepper put it, it took some time but the payoff was amazing. The pair appeared in buildings all over New York City, performing at the opening ceremonies and parties for their more well-known counterparts. Mr. Petersen was planning some kind of promotion party for Pepper and Molly along with some of the important people in the radio business, and Molly and Pepper both could hardly wait.

A few people even knew who they were when they walked down the streets together, calling out to Molly and Pepper. Molly always waved hello but Pepper almost always wanted to talk to people.

Something in her just knew it wasn't good for Pepper to be so popular, she wondered how long it would be till it all got to his head. Molly worried about him as she watched him talk and joke with people, they were earning a decent living, and there was nothing wrong with that, but too much money could ruin people. Would Pepper continue to still be the old Pepper that she knew, or would he be corrupted and changed into something completely different? *Only time will tell*, she thought, and shuddered.

Molly stood talking to a woman while the crew set up chairs, tables and devices that would be needed for the performance. Mr. Petersen came up beside her.

"Hello Molly," he said with a smile. "Are you ready to play?"

Molly looked up to him and nodded while saying, "Sure am."

He put a hand on her shoulder. "Make it good, Molly," he said as he looked around the building, "there are producers here, there are big names here, and there are tons of advertisers here. You never know what can happen with all these people."

The woman that had been talking to Molly excused herself and then left. Molly continued to look around the large room that they were in, decorated festively in preparation for what was to come. Tables were set up with food and drinks covering them and decorations were even on the walls; there were a few people standing around but the majority of the people would not arrive for another hour.

Molly sighed. "Yep."

"You've done an amazing job so far Molly. I know you are a bit on the shy side, but I know that there's a part of you that wants the limelight too. And I've seen that part come out now, keep it coming girl! You're special and I know it. Just don't let that Pepper steal all the attention."

Molly grinned at him and nodded knowingly.

"Speaking of Pepper," he continued, "have you seen that kid around lately? He simply cannot be late for the performance."

"I think he was over near the entrance smoking with some guys," Molly said.

"Was he smoking Lucky Strikes?" he asked quickly.

"I don't know," Molly said, "I think so."

"That boy can't smoke anything else or our advertisers will be disappointed. I'll have to make sure those are!" He turned to go find Pepper and started away, but then stopped.

"And do me a favor," he said. "Keep an eye on Pepper," he said in a serious tone. "It's going to be a long night and I don't want him drinking. Especially not in front of these guys."

Molly looked at him again and nodded but didn't say anything.

"But man, that kid can be contrary and defiant," he said and then left.

"I agree," Molly said under her breath, "one hundred percent."

Not too long after, Molly was on the stage, Pepper beside her with his polished new guitar. Molly gave Pepper a signal behind her back and they introduced themselves to the crowd in front of them, and began with a slower song that they could both take turns singing to. Molly looked over her violin to see Pepper up in front of her singing into the microphone with his deep voice that she liked so much. When his part of the song was over he looked over his shoulder at Molly and grinned ear to ear, then backed away for Molly's turn.

Molly stepped up to the mike and her voice poured out into the microphone and was amplified all over the room, sounding sweeter to her ears then she had ever remembered. As she looked around to the large audience in front of her, she tried not to let her voice crack as her legs began to get a little shaky. *I'm not nervous,* she told herself, *not nervous at all.*

She looked into the eyes of her audience, smiled and sang as loudly as she possibly could. Time seemed to move differently, as it always did when she played, but in a different way. Her eyes shone as she glanced to the shimmering lights and then down to her short, shimmery blue dress and her high-heeled shoes that she had just recently become accustomed to walking in.

She didn't really think too much about it, but she suddenly realized just how silly all of this would have seemed to her only a few months ago. Her eyes glanced to Pepper and how out of place he looked in a suit, his unruly hair slicked back like a true gentleman.

Before she knew it, though, the song was over and they moved on to the next and then took a break to mingle with some of the people who had come to the occasion. She stood next to the table full of treats and grabbed a cup of punch.

"Hello there."

Molly turned to see a young tall redheaded woman in a long emerald green dress addressing her and Molly smiled.

"Oh and if you don't mind . . ." the woman reached up and adjusted Molly's elegant brunette bun, tucking in some stray hairs that had fallen out and fluffing the curls around her face.

She smiled at Molly. "My name's Margret, and I know that you're Molly. So how long have you been in the radio business?" she asked kindly.

"About six weeks," Molly answered.

"That's nice," she said, "I'm actually from Hollywood but I'm on a kind of tour thing here and my agent thought it would be good if I stopped here with him."

Molly nodded.

"You're such a sweet thing," Margret told her, "it's no wonder everyone loves you." She took a sip from her glass of punch.

"And that Pepper," she said with a laugh. "He's such a character."

Molly followed her gaze and found Pepper standing in a group of men, holding a glass in one hand and explaining something animatedly with the other, laughing hysterically every now and then.

She frowned at him, but then turned to Margret and asked, "So what's it like, the movie business?"

Margret raised her eyebrows and her green eyes seemed to sparkle. "It's hard work. Nothing like what you have to do, like come into a station every week or month or whatever and just promote yourselves. Every day we're up at five for twelve or thirteen-hour days. We have to wear tons of makeup and it's hot and sweaty inside the studio and you get yelled at a lot. But I wouldn't trade it for the world! I'm aspiring to be a real movie star someday, not just a boring old extra!"

Molly smiled and nodded in agreement. "That would be nice." Just then she looked over some people's shoulders to see Mr. Petersen gesturing frantically in her direction.

"But I'd better go," she said to Margret. "I guess I'm supposed to meet somebody."

"Well I'm in town for a couple months, so I'll have someone give your agent my number if you ever want to talk."

The two smiled at each other and then Molly left. "Who's that?" Mr. Petersen asked her as she approached him.

"Oh," Molly said, "that's Margret. She's a girl from Hollywood."

Mr. Petersen just stared after her. "Well, anyway, it's good that you get to know as many influential people as possible, Molly. But right now we need to get you back up on the stage again. Apparently they are going to get you two some more backup instruments."

Molly sighed exasperatedly. "But it's almost ten o'clock already. It's getting late and I want to go home."

Mr. Petersen stopped looking around and looked back at Molly. "You need to stay, honey, at least until this last part is over."

Mr. Petersen found Pepper at last standing in a group of men. "And did I tell you about the time Molly out-fiddled some other stuck-up girl in Indiana? Wait, is out-fiddled even a word? But anyway, it was amazing! Sometimes I wish we could go back to those times when we fought out a living, but--"

"You need to get ready for your next performance, Pepper," Mr. Petersen informed Pepper. Pepper sighed and slicked his hair back, said goodbye to the guys and followed Molly up to the stage.

The pair climbed up the few stairs in the back of the stage where a few other men picked up instruments to play. Molly looked around the stage to see a bass player, another guitarist, a mandolin and a banjo. She smiled to herself and picked up her violin, peering over to the crowd that was now mostly seated in front of her.

"What song are we playin?" she turned and asked.

"Well," one of the guys said, "Mr. Petersen said that you guys knew the song 'Foggy Mountain Breakdown' so we thought that maybe we could play that."

"Sure thing!" said Pepper, and started out the chord sequence. The next instant, the men around had joined in and Molly grinned and pulled her violin in too.

She loved the song, it was on the faster side and it had a break in for each instrument to play their own little solo. Each person played their own instument's part until the song was finished with Pepper's guitar.

Pepper swung his guitar in front of him, gently shoved Molly out of the way and moved to the mike. "We're gonna play that song 'Lulu Walls'!" The crowd began to cheer. Pepper turned around and smiled at Molly, catching her eyes. "That alright baby?" he asked.

But Molly cringed slightly when she made eye contact with him. Something wasn't right about him. His soft brown eyes were red-rimmed and he didn't quite smile the way he usually did. But Molly looked away and began to play the song, even though she didn't particularly like it.

Pepper did the singing himself and didn't let Molly get near the mike. She was okay with that though because the song was a fast song that was mostly about some man wanting a stubborn girl and her voice didn't seem to fit the song. But when Pepper began playing notes with his guitar instead of chords and taking over the main part of the song, Molly began to get a little peeved.

"One evening getting dark, we first met at the park,
Sitting by the fountain all alone
I lifted my hat, and then began to chat
She said she'd 'low me to see her at her home.

Such a star I've never seen, she's as perty as a queen!
She's as perfect as an angel from above
If she'd only be my wife, I'd live happy all my life
With that aggravating beauty Lulu Walls.

Pepper sang out the first two verses, getting louder as he went along. Molly knew that Pepper was a natural showoff, but this was unusual for even him. Most of the mass of people now were clapping together with the beat, and the entire atmosphere of the room was buzzing with excitement. Some of the crowd was standing on their chairs, cheering Pepper on through the song. Molly retreated to the back of the stage, her fiddle playing sounding softer as Pepper became more rowdy with his guitar.

If she were only mine, I would build a house so fine
And around it so many fences tall
It would make me jealous free, that no one else but me
Could gaze upon that beauty Lulu Walls

One evening getting late, I met her at the gate
I'd asked her if she'd wed me in the fall
She only turned away, and nothing would she say
That aggravating beauty Lulu Walls!

 Pepper threw his arm up and sang his lungs out, and the crowd could feel that he was putting his entire soul into his performance, and they cheered wildly. Before he or Molly knew it a tall blonde girl had climbed the stage and kissed Pepper right on the lips in front of everyone on the stage.

 Molly could hardly believe her eyes. Pepper's hands stayed on his guitar and his eyes closed gently as he accepted the kiss from a complete stranger.

 Molly's hands felt limp as she barely finished out the song. When the song was over she put her violin away behind stage and fled out of the building, back towards home. Or what it was that she now called home.

 She ran nearly the entire way there, down the dark streets of New York City to the building where she and Pepper lived. She pulled her set of keys out of her evening bag and opened the door to their apartment, then ran inside and flopped down on the bed, sobbing.

Pepper pulled away from the tall beauty in a daze, barely noticing Molly throw her fiddle in its case and flee out of the room. The crowd cheered loudly and he took a bow then put his instrument away and made his way offstage, his head throbbing with every step.

"Yeah!" his group of guys cheered him on when he was back with them, and another glass was put into his hand. "That's the way to play the gee-tar!" He guzzled the drink down and grinned at his counterparts, then began to say something when he felt someone's hand on his shoulder.

He turned to see the blonde girl who had climbed onto the stage with him. She smiled at him, her lips as red as roses and her shining eyes lined in thick black makeup. "So do you think that you could spend the night with me?"

Pepper's eyes widened. "Well, actually," he started, tripping over his words. "I have someone already who, who-- Molly? Where's Molly at?"

At that moment Mr. Petersen walked up behind them. "Pepper! Where is Molly? I saw her leave but I don't know where she went. Are you going to go find her?"

"Well, can I at least get your number?" the tall blonde girl asked.

But Pepper was looking around himself now, trying desperately to locate Molly, as that seemed to be all that mattered to him at this moment. His eyes turned to the exit, and he turned to run out the door without answering the girl's question.

Molly woke up with a start when she heard keys fumbling outside of the door. She lifted her head off her damp pillow and looked toward the door. *Pepper!* She thought angrily, and scooted forward to sit up on her bed.

"Molly?" Pepper inquired as he stuck his head inside the door. *Umph!*

Molly hurled a pillow into his face, throwing him off balance and he nearly fell to the floor but grabbed for the dresser.

She lashed out a string of curse words at him, then stuffed her head under her pillow again.

"Molly, I know it looked like I was really havin' it with that girl, but, but, but . . ." he stammered.

"You're drunk."

Pepper stopped talking and looked toward the ground, silent. Quietly he took out a pack of Lucky Strikes and lit one up, inhaling a deep puff and staring at the wall.

The two stayed silently like that for a good ten minutes, Molly lying in bed peeking under her pillow at Pepper, who stood leaning against the wall saying nothing. Finally Pepper threw it away and sat beside Molly on the bed.

He took her hand in his and stroked it softly, and Molly turned to look at him with tears glistening in her eyes. "Listen Molly," he said. "I know I can be kind of unruly sometimes and you'd rather I just calm down and listen to you all the time. I can't change, but I promise you that I'll try to keep myself on the good side of things and I'll behave myself. And I do know one thing: I love you."

Molly wiped a tear from her eye and sniffled, and looked up to Pepper. His eyes were red and tired, but sincere, and so she smiled. She closed her eyes and rested her head against his strong shoulder, simply exhausted from the busy night and from all the stress that performing had put her under. Pepper sat there with her for a moment, stroking her dark brown hair.

"And that's why I got you this," he said, and pulled something out of the pocket of his suit. Molly's eyes grew large as she saw the little black case, and he opened it gingerly, pulling the ring out from the inside. He picked up her hand and slipped it on her ring finger. "I know you think I'm immature and unruly and wild, but . . ."

Molly's eyes met his again and Pepper smiled. "Will you marry me?"

She sniffled, laughed and then said, "It's two-thirty in the morning Pepper and you're asking me to marry you?"

"Of course."

"But what about all your talk about being wild and free on the road and all that? You're only a teenager and I thought that you didn't want to be married and tied down and all that jazz."

"But when I said that I never would have guessed in a million years that I would meet someone as special as you. You made me change my mind, Molly."

Molly looked into his expressive dark brown eyes again and almost began to cry all over again. "But you know that I'll never tie you down. I love adventure and freedom just as much as you do."

"I know that."

"And there's no one else that I'd rather have the adventure with. So of course I will!" She smiled at him.

Pepper held her hands, gazing into her eyes as his face lit up with an even bigger smile. "And I've got another surprise."

"What?" Molly began to say, but Pepper pulled her hand, leading her out of their apartment, down the elevator, and across the lobby of their building.

"Alright," Pepper said, smiling. "Close your eyes. Shut them tight!"

He led her across the street and into a more secluded parking area. He stopped and put his hand on Molly's shoulder. "Alright. Open them!"

Molly opened her eyes to see a shiny black Model A parked in front of her, and she gasped. "Pepper!" was all she managed to say.

"Now we can hop in our own car and drive wherever we want! No more riding the rails, no more hitching rides, and no more walking for miles and miles!"

"It's beautiful," Molly managed to say. "But it makes me kinda sad, too."

"Why is that?" Pepper asked.

"Just because," Molly answered, "it seems like our carefree life is over now. I mean, traveling was what we were really all about."

"Our carefree life is just beginning!" Pepper told her, grasping her hands tightly and refusing to let his eyes leave hers. "If we can keep riding this wave of prosperity, who knows how far we'll go? I think that it is time for us to move on now, Molly. It's time to start a new phase of our lives."

"Aright," Molly answered quietly. "I trust you, Pepper."

Pepper felt a shiver run down his back when she said that. He knew that even though she had never said it, Molly had a hard time trusting people. Anyone. But she had said it outright to him.

Pepper looked down to the ground, then back up at Molly. "You know my real name isn't Pepper."

Molly burst out laughing. "Of course I know that!"

"Well, do you want to know what my real name is?"

Molly smiled. "Well it wouldn't hurt to know. But I guess if we are going to be husband and wife I should know!"

"Daniel." Pepper stated simply. "Daniel Thompson."

Molly pulled away from Pepper and took a good look at him. "Daniel, eh?" She scratched an eyebrow. "You actually kind of look like a Daniel. But I just have to keep calling you Pepper. I've never known you by anything else."

Pepper looked at her and smiled, then broke into a laugh. Molly smiled as she watched Pepper, then broke into a giggle herself. She moved her body closer to Pepper and put a hand on his chest. Under the lights of New York City, Pepper closed his eyes, leaned down and kissed Molly's lips tenderly. Sometime later Molly opened her eyes and pulled away, gazing into Pepper's dark eyes. "We're both so tired, it's been a really long day. I'm exhausted. I think it's time for bed."

Pepper nodded in agreement, too tired to say anything else as he reached for her hand once again and then made their way back to the apartment building.

Chapter 11

"You're getting married?!" The voice held an incredulous tone.

Pepper frowned at Mr. Petersen. "Um, yes. Is that necessarily a bad thing?"

Molly sat next to Pepper on a soft flowery sofa in the lobby of their apartment building, Mr. Petersen sat on a matching chair opposite from them with a look of surprise written on his face.

"But you're only teenagers! Don't you think you need some time to wait and think about it?" he asked incredulously.

"Would you like some soda?" a lady asked them as she passed.

"No, thank you," Mr. Petersen shot at her, irritated at the interruption. She only shrugged her shoulders and left.

"You can't get married now, your schedule simply won't allow for it," he continued. When the two said nothing he kept on, "Pepper, can I talk to you? Privately?"

Pepper shrugged. "Sure."

"Come with me then." Mr. Petersen gestured for Pepper to follow, and Pepper stood from the couch and left Molly.

When they reached a more private room, he stopped. "Are you sure you want to do this?" he asked.

"Of course."

"But you just don't seem like the type! You're sure you want to be a married man? You probably don't know what you're in for . . ."

"I've held Molly in suspense for long enough," Pepper said. "Besides, I love her." He looked back in Molly's direction.

Mr. Petersen sighed and turned away. "If you feel that way, I guess there is nothing I can do. But you must wait until a time when you two are less busy. We've got recordings and appearances scheduled on nearly every day from now until sometime this spring. I don't know when we'll have time for a wedding!"

"But it will just be a small one," Pepper said. "Molly and I don't have a lot of friends in New York anyway."

"Why, everyone who listens to the radio Thursday nights is your friend! I can't imagine the publicity that would result from the matter. But think about it, Pepper," Mr. Petersen said, turning back to make eye contact with Pepper. "You have an image to upkeep. Everybody glamorizes about your carefree lifestyle, and you may damper it somewhat by letting people know that you've tied the knot already."

Pepper face darkened into a scowl. "Well, Mr. Petersen, you should know by now that this is my life and I intend to live it anyway I please. The radio audience is important to me, but I'm not going to let them influence every decision I make."

And with that he rushed out of the room, leaving the confused Mr. Petersen to himself.

"Come on, Molly," he said, quickly walking past the couch where he had left her. Molly rose to follow him.

"Where are we going?" She asked.

"We're just going on a little walk," Pepper said, grabbing a jacket. "I'm tired of all this business talk anyway."

The pair stepped out of the building and out into the cool November air. Molly's spirits lifted the second she was outside, and she took notice of her surroundings as she walked at Pepper's side.

Immediately her ears were filled with the sounds of a busy city; cars and trucks growling down the road and honking at each other, men's voices calling out to each other from the streets and construction sites in the area, and people shouting out advertisements for their wares on the street corners.

Smog hung over the city as it usually did, but through it Molly noticed a few beautiful snowflakes falling from the gray sky. She stopped in the middle of the large sidewalk and held out a hand, seemingly unaware of the pedestrian traffic all around her. Pepper watched as a snowflake landed on her hand and then as she brought it up to her face.

Pepper shivered a bit and pulled his newsboy cap tighter down on his head. He then subconsciously wrapped his jacket tighter around him as he watched Molly, and looked ahead on the street.

"Can you imagine?" Molly said, "what it would be like if we were still riding the rails or in New York City looking for work or a place to play?"

"It would be mighty cold," he said.

Molly smiled. "And it's only November. I don't know what we would do once it got into December and January. We might have starved or frozen to death."

Pepper tucked his head down and began walking against the wind. "I can't wait until I get my license and then we can drive wherever we want."

"Well how are you going to pass that test and get your license when you can't even read?" Molly asked, then laughed but instantly regretted it.

Pepper grinned anyway. "I was kind of hoping that you would help me with that."

It was silent for a moment while Molly and Pepper continued to walk down the New York sidewalk, enjoying the scenery and taking in the bustling surroundings. As they walked deeper into the city they began to see taller industrial buildings and even more activity swarming around them. Molly wondered how it was that Pepper never did get lost when they walked through the city.

A little boy selling newspapers on a street corner caught Molly's eye. Nearly four feet tall, he looked much too small to be out attempting to make money, but already he did a good job of it calling out the headlines.

"You can't hear this on the darned radio!" he called out sharply, "Yessir, this stuff is fresh!"

Molly smiled when she looked into his little blue eyes, taking notice of the freckles slapped across his tanned face and the cute little gap between his front teeth. His clothes were tattered and worn, but the boy seemed to be warm enough in the cold weather. He reminded Molly of someone she knew. Suddenly though her smile faded as she remembered who that someone was. The little boy looked just like her brother Thomas.

She shivered, not so much from the wind but from the memories that were swirling around in her head. Taking a deep breath, she moved closer to Pepper and slipped her hand in his. He turned to her and smiled, but suddenly his attention was turned to a scene playing out in front of them.

She heard shouts from men as they marched in front of a factory just outside of its gates.

"Look!" Pepper said to her, "They're on strike! And not just a sit-down strike, but a full-blown march! Let's go in and see if they get into any fights." An excited looked filled his brown eyes as he looked over the crowd of people that was forming, and he began to make his way over toward them.

"No!" Molly started. "I mean, it was just plain lady luck that got us out of the joint the first time, and now you're going to put us right back in there."

He stopped and looked at her, eyebrow raised. "We won't get into trouble," he said. "I promise."

Molly just sighed, and followed him into the crowd. "Yeah, right," she mumbled to herself. "That's what you always say."

"Oh boy," Pepper said, pushing his way through the people. "Lookit that!"

Molly saw mostly men in patched clothing who were yelling and tossing things at the building. There was an illegal fire built in the middle of the street to keep the protesters warm from the biting November wind. People standing outside held big white wooden signs with slogans painted in tall, dark letters.

She didn't like it. Molly could sense that there was a fight brewing only a few minutes away. A few cops had lined up on the side on the crowd, holding containers of what Molly guessed was something like mace or tear gas. Somehow Molly had allowed Pepper's hand to slip from hers, and she tried to keep her eyes on Pepper's carrot-colored hair standing out above the crowd.

It was only a few minutes later when Molly lost him and gave up looking for him, feeling especially small and lonely in the huge crowd. Pulling her jacket closer around her, she comforted herself by remembering that Pepper had an amazing ability to locate her whenever they had gotten separated and Molly relaxed a bit.

Suddenly Molly heard a banging sound ahead of her, followed by a noise that sounded like a sharp shot.

BANG!

She heard it again.

Not again, she thought, unwisely pushing herself toward the front of the crowd where she last saw Pepper heading.

Not thirty seconds later the two sides collided. Molly didn't know how it all started, but she saw the police coming after the workers in a furious line, attempting to chase them away from the factory. The opposing workers charged in a livid mess of arms, legs, and homemade weapons.

At first it seemed as if the workers were winning, for they surely outnumbered the cops by a great deal. Molly found herself caught right in the middle of the mess, desperately trying to find Pepper but trying not to get involved in the chaos around her. Her head throbbed and she felt the sting of a misplaced arm as it cracked against her head.

She held her fury inside this time though. Molly gave up on searching for Pepper and attempted to hightail out of there and get back to the safety of the apartment. Pepper would be able to have his little fight and then get home hopefully without injuring himself too badly.

*Haha, **little**.* Molly thought again. *How did Pepper always manage to get into so much trouble? And what's more, seem to enjoy it?*

At that precise moment Molly caught sight of Pepper, whacking officers left and right with a swollen right eye but huge grin on his face.

"Pepper!" Molly called, running toward him and trying to get his attention. They had to get out of there.

Molly shoved people even harder, focusing her eyes and all of her energy on getting to Pepper and then getting out of there. She felt the strong urge to join in the fight but she knew that she couldn't, and shouldn't. They weren't tramps anymore; they had real jobs and they were above this!

Molly was so close to Pepper that she had reached out to grab his hand. But the cops were winning now, and were mercilessly chasing the majority of the workers away from the factory. With a thud of bodies colliding, a burly man ran obliviously into Molly's smaller form. Molly felt her feet swept out from under her and threw her hands backward to catch herself. Another man ran into the first, and Molly was thrown to the ground.

With a sickening crack she landed on her right hand and felt her wrist bend backward. She cried out in pain and the men stood to their feet and ran harder away from the madness.

She saw Pepper running away from the scene toward her, the police following only a short distance behind. Quickly standing to her feet, she held her limp hand with the other, and called out to him again. He ran past her, grabbing the edge of her long coat and pulling her along with him, a hint of fear showing in his brown eyes.

The officers ran after them, showing no pity for the fact that she was a girl or that she was hurt. Pepper was a fast runner and kept Molly at his side. They were soon huffing and puffing, but far ahead of their pursuers. Pepper stopped briefly and turned to them, arrogantly shouting, "You'll be sorry! You should know that we are actually prominent radio personalities and won't let this—"

They responded readily by shooting him in the butt with a salt pellet gun. The blast only infuriated Pepper even more and he let out a string of curse words directed at the officers before Molly grabbed him with her good hand and pulled him away.

Chapter 12

LOCAL RADIO PERSONALITIES MOLLY MORGAN AND DANIEL "PEPPER" TOMPSON INVOLVED IN DOWNTOWN STREET FIGHT

"What is this!?" Mr. Petersen practically yelled in the hospital room. "What is this!?"

He began to read:

"Molly Morgan and her infamous partner 'Pepper' were spotted Friday afternoon observing the proceedings of factory workers on strike in downtown NY. Though it was not apparent that they were involved with the strike or what the pair was doing in that part of town, sources say that they appeared in the crowd shortly before the fight broke out. Officers from Brown Department were stationed on the sidelines to keep the peace.

It is not known who started the fight, but it was said that one of the workers threw an object at the officers to begin the brawl. 'I thought that those two looked kind of familiar,' Mr. Wells, one of the officers, said."

"Yeah, sure you did," Pepper interrupted, "I know you thought about that when you went ahead and shot me in the bum."

Mr. Petersen gave him a look and then continued reading.

"'Though they are on the radio, it's not like we see their faces every day, so I guess most of us had no idea who they were.'

Witnesses say that Pepper was involved in the brawl; it wasn't confirmed whether Morgan was or not but she has been injured and was taken to a hospital shortly after the fight."

Mr. Petersen shook the paper and then folded it neatly, his anger held back.

"They can't ever get my last name right!" Molly whined.

"And whose fault it that?" Mr. Petersen shot back, irritated.

Molly sat on a hospital bed, her wrist bound tight in a cast, with Pepper sitting beside her in a chair.

"The author probably made it up because they have no records on your true last name," Mr. Petersen continued, "at least they got the right paperwork on your name, Pepper."

Pepper had his head in his hands now, pulling his fingers through his hair and looking a little frazzled. There was a long cut along his jawline, and his eye was dark and puffy again.

Molly felt so upset that she could feel her stomach sinking; she felt as if she had let Mr. Petersen down and it made her feel terrible. She wasn't sure about Pepper but he seemed to be feeling the same way. But what really troubled her was her wrist. She lifted the cast up and took a long, hard look at it.

Pepper noticed her movement and looked up, hair rumpled. He knew as well as she did that she wouldn't be able to play the fiddle with a broken wrist.

Molly ran her fingers along the cast again and shivered, remembering the little bit of white bone that had been sticking out at such an odd angle. She halfheartedly sniffed at it, then wrinkled her nose. It reeked of the salve that the nurses had put on it. It was nicely taken care of by the staff at the hospital, but it was still very painful.

Mr. Petersen heaved a long, heavy sigh. "Doctor said that you probably won't be able to play for at least six weeks."

Pepper shook his head and Molly held back hot tears.

"You'll be able to go home later this afternoon, though, so be thankful for that." With that, he stood to his feet and motioned for Pepper to follow him. Pepper gave her a quick kiss, then followed Mr. Petersen out of the room. Molly leaned back in her bed and let loose the tears.

"Molly. Molly!"

Molly was shaken awake by Pepper a few days later. She sat up out of her bed in their apartment and rubbed her head, looking to the clock.

"You're sure up early. What's going on?" she asked him.

He grinned. "Mr. Petersen has a plan."

She turned her head a little and smiled at him curiously. "And what is that?"

"Well, the show must go on," Pepper pretended to straighten an imaginary tie and imitated Mr. Petersen expertly. Molly laughed. "So he has a plan."

"Spit it out already!" Molly begged him.

"He's got someone else to play the fiddle for you."

The smile on Molly's face fell and she looked puzzled. "What—" she began, but was interrupted.

"He says that you can come to the studio and just talk, and that he'll have someone else play the fiddle for ya for a few weeks 'cause we're on the radio and no one will know the difference."

"But isn't that deceitful?" she asked him.

"Naa," he replied casually. "They'll never know!"

Molly looked doubtful, but just shrugged it off. Mr. Petersen was their agent, so he should probably know what he was doing, she guessed.

Molly rubbed her cast again, wishing so hard that she would be able to take if off soon. Her eyes fell to the shelf where she kept her violin and she sighed. She looked around the room where she stayed, the room that was really was her own room in her own apartment and back to Pepper.

He had a huge grin on his freckled face, his hair was at least partially combed that morning, and his brown eyes sparkled as he talked to her. But none of that was what Molly was really thinking about.

"Pepper?" she asked cautiously.

"Yeah?"

"Do you ever wonder, like how's your family doing?" She paused for a moment before continuing. Family. The word was so hard for her to say, and it felt like a strange taste in her mouth. "I know that you're family really isn't around, but you've got to have some extended relatives, or something. Someone to go back to."

When he didn't say anything Molly kept on. "I didn't think that I was very close to my mother and father, or my brothers. But the longer I've been away, the more I think about them. Where are they now? What are they doing? Do they know anything about what we're doing? Should I try to find them?" Molly sighed and looked down.

Pepper thought for a moment and then took hold of Molly's hand. "Look at me, Molly. Look at this. This is your life now. *We* are a family. Just me and you."

Molly looked down to Pepper's hand entwined in her own, and thought about everything that had gone on between them from when they first met. She raised her eyes to meet his; his dark brown eyes that seemed to be able to mesmerize her. The eyes that always held her gaze and that didn't dart away from hers like so many others boys'.

"I'm not sure what you're thinking, but if your parents haven't come looking for you yet then they probably never will. Molly, we've got each other now and that's got to be enough."

He tucked a piece of her hair behind her ear. "Wouldn't it be crazy if we had a baby though? Mr. Petersen would be ticked."

Molly burst out laughing and Pepper raised his eyebrows. "What? What's so funny about that? I'm serious."

"Oh, I don't know," Molly told him, "It's just the way you said it." And she giggled some more, with Pepper finally joining in.

"I don't know what we would call him," Molly said. "Though we could always name him after you. We could call him Trouble, with a capital T!"

They laughed some more, until Pepper pulled Molly up and carefully spun her around, saying, "Come on, let's go. There's so much to do today! And Mr. Petersen says that we can try out that shiny new Model A." Molly looked worried. "Don't be scared, Molly, I promise I'll be careful!"

"Pepper! Slow down!"

Pepper laughed and pushed the accelerator down harder, resulting in a screech from Molly. "Calm down!" he laughed, "we're not even going thirty-five yet!"

Pepper held tightly to the wheel of the fancy black car with both hands, grinning hugely as he spun around another corner, throwing up a spray of gravel and dust. Molly sat shotgun beside him, her casted hand in her lap and her left hand gripping the edge of the seat fearfully.

Mr. Petersen had someone take them out far away from the city of New York, where there were plenty of dirt roads and thankfully not many pedestrians. "Have fun," the man had said before he left them to figure out how to drive by themselves, "and don't get hurt!"

Molly considered that a real possibility as she braced her feet harder against the floor, as if it would help. She didn't even know if this was legal. Pepper downshifted, then leaned back and casually draped one hand on the wheel. "I don't know what all the hype is about these automobiles, anyway," he said. "Driving is easy."

Molly didn't say anything but looked back behind them into the cloud of dust following them, her hair whipping annoyingly into her face and eyes. Who would've guessed that they would have gone from common street tramps, hobos really, to being on the radio? She couldn't believe it, but there they were, driving along the road in their very own car.

"That Mr. Fairlaine does a pretty good job at the fiddle," Pepper said, breaking into her thoughts.

Molly looked up from the window and back to Pepper. "But I still don't like it," she continued, "I don't like having someone else playing for me. What if the newspapers catch wind of it? It could be the end of us. Everyone who listens to us would be disappointed."

"We just gotta lay low for awhile," Pepper pointed out. "We'll be alright as long as we don't try to attract any extra attention."

Molly moved her fingers outside of the cast, feeling sulky that she would not be able to use her hand for another month or so. She felt like pointing out the fact that it was really Pepper's fault all along that she was injured. But suddenly she noticed a figure walking along the road.

"Look over there," she said, pointing. Pepper followed her gaze and saw the traveler as well.

"Should we pick him up?" he asked.

A shadow of caution crossed Molly's mind before she answered, but she ignored it. "Why not?"

Pepper pulled over beside the man. "Need a ride?" he asked. The man nodded and climbed in the back of the car. When Pepper heard the door slam he jolted ahead.

"Where you heading?" Pepper asked.

"I really don't know," the man answered. "South probably. I'm just a traveler. A hobo, really."

"Well, that's exactly what me and Molly here used to be!" Pepper said.

Molly turned around in her seat to get a better look at the man. He had a few years on herself and Pepper, but he was still fairly young. He had short brown hair and the beginnings of a beard growing, with a sharp, jutting face and interesting features. He wore patchy overalls with a dirty tan shirt underneath, and he didn't smell the best but seemed like he was a friendly man nonetheless.

"My name is Brett." He said simply. "I didn't hear your names though."

Pepper tried to keep his eyes on the road but kept looking back to the man as he talked to him. "Well, I'm Pepper, and this here is Molly. She's my fiancé; we're officially getting married in a few months," he explained.

Brett nodded. "So how did you two get out of travelin'?" he asked simply as he stared out of the window.

"It's kind of a long story. But we got into the radio business instead," Pepper boasted.

The man raised an eyebrow. "Hmm, really," he noted quietly but didn't investigate further, so Pepper didn't say anything else about it.

"Is there any particular place you want to go? I mean, Molly and I aren't really going anywhere. This is actually my first driving lesson, and I'm kinda teaching myself out here away from the city. We're just supposed to be back at the tavern before nightfall."

"I'm not sure," Brett said quietly. "I'm actually heading down south to a small town called Roseville. Jimmy and the gang are down there waitin' for me. They're gonna get something big this time."

Pepper raised his eyebrows and looked at Molly, then back to the man. "What kinda business are you into, Brett?" he asked.

The man looked down toward his shoes, but up again at Pepper. "The devil's business," he said.

Pepper grinned and asked enthusiastically, "You mean stealin' stuff? Robbing banks? Holdin' up stores?"

The man had seemed quiet and reserved, but seeing Pepper's obvious interest he gained a little confidence and laughed. "Sort of," he replied. Pepper looked back over the seat again, excited. "We used to be into robbin' banks and the such, but things have gotten a little slippery with the cops around here."

"Serves them right, anyway, for taking everyone's money like that anyway," Pepper said. "Pssh, who ever heard of a bank holiday anyway?"

Molly felt like slapping Pepper. She knew that the banks were generally frowned upon and that robbers were made out to be Robin Hood-like heroes in this day and age but two wrongs didn't make a right, and Pepper should have known that.

"We've just gotten into sellin' stuff now. But we do occasionally stick up places."

Pepper slowed down to avoid a large nearly feral herd of cattle crossing the road, and then stopped, waiting for them to move out of the way. "Gosh, I'm kinda hungry," Brett said. "Got any food in here?"

"We packed some food for a sort of picnic I guess," Pepper answered, his eyes on the cows ahead of him. "In case we don't come to a town for a while."

"Well, why don't you stop up here in this next pasture and we sit out and eat?" he asked. "We can always sit in the car if it gets too cold."

Pepper nodded. "Sure we can. We have plenty to share."

When they came across another pasture with an open fence, Pepper turned in and parked the Ford under a small grove of trees.

All three of them stepped out of the car and Molly went to the backseat to grab the bag they had filled with food. She laid down a blanket for them to sit on and then pulled out the food that had been carefully packed for them. There was cold turkey sandwiches, apple juice and ginger ale, watermelon, an assortment of vegetables and a peach cake neatly folded up in a towel for dessert. Molly sat down underneath the huge tree and arranged some food on her napkin and just about had it up to her mouth when the man suddenly interrupted her.

"Should we say grace?" He asked, but the way he said it made it sound more like a demand than a question. He bowed his head and Molly looked to Pepper, who shrugged but then put his food down and folded his hands.

"Dear Father in heaven," the man started. Molly opened her eyes just the tiniest bit to observe the man praying. His eyes were fully closed and he continued on earnestly.

"We thank you this day for this meal that you have given us. Thank you for keeping your hands of protection around us, for keeping us safe and sound in this ungodly world. And Father God, I thank you for these two friends that you've brought to me and for the gift of time we have. Amen."

Molly's eyes immediately popped open and she looked to Brett, unable to keep her gaze off him. How could he be such a hypocrite? Praying and acting all Christian then stealing and robbing, and maybe even killing? The man eyed the food greedily but ate an appropriate portion. When he was finished he sat with his back against a thick tree, with his hands playing with the holes in the pockets in his jacket.

Molly packed the food back into the bag, watching Pepper and Brett talk to each other about what they had gotten away with in the past. She saw Pepper's eyes light up with something like excitement as he talked to the man.

"You know what we should do?" Brett asked, pulling out a gun out of his jacket. Molly instinctively jumped backwards.

"Whoa!" Pepper exclaimed with a whistle. "Nice pistol!"

"Target practice," Brett explained with a smile. "Got anything we can shoot at?"

Pepper shook his head slowly, but then began, "We have a couple of old cans. Oh, and this black and white promo poster of Molly and me. That would be fun to shoot at."

Molly frowned and continued to pack up the leftovers. The two men left and shortly after Molly heard the loud, sharp shots pinging into the tin cans and then burring themselves into the tree where Pepper had hung the poster. When she was finished she hopped in the car and shut the door in an attempt to get away from the chilly air outside.

"Come on, Molly!" she heard Pepper call out, and he waved to her. "Come over here and try it out yourself! I know you'll like it."

Molly hopped out of the car and walked over to where they were standing in the field. "How I am supposed to hold it with this?" she asked, pointing at her cast.

"Don't worry about it," Pepper told her, "you can hold it in your left hand and then you'll have an excuse for when you miss everything."

Molly shrugged. She wasn't afraid of guns, but it wasn't exactly her favorite thing to do. As the two rearranged the tin cans and straightened the poster, she tried to think back to the last time she had used a gun. She had been little, for sure. Molly thought that it was probably about the time she was thirteen, and she remembered how proud her father had been when she shot a squirrel out of an old oak tree from a good distance.

"Over here, Molly," Brett said, motioning to where he wanted her to stand. Molly shook the memory from her head and stood next to Brett. "Here you go," he said, placing the pistol into her hand. "Hold it tight," he warned. "It's gonna kick a bit but you look like a tough little girl."

Molly looked ahead to the small poster pinned up on the tree. It was a black and white photograph, a picture of Pepper standing with his hand in front of him resting on the top of his guitar, herself standing next to him with a huge smile, fiddle in one hand, bow in the other. Both of their signatures graced the bottom.

She aimed carefully, looking towards the poster. It was such a shame to have to shoot themselves, but it was either herself or him. She grinned and chose Pepper, and squeezed the trigger with a huge blast. Her left wrist wasn't exactly ready for the kick from the strong gun, and it shot backwards but Molly barely kept control. Molly was glad that playing the fiddle required both hands to be strong.

"Ya' shot me in the nose!" Pepper yelled, and Brett broke out into laughter.

Molly just smiled and cocked the gun again. She was beginning to like this. *Bang, bang, ping!* She shot two of the three tin cans that stood on top of fence posts, and barely nicked the third one.

Brett just gaped in amazement. "Where'd you learn to shoot like that?" he asked incredulously, "you're not left-handed, are you?"

Molly shook her head. "It's a talent that runs in the family," Molly said coolly. "Well at least that's what I've been told."

She turned and looked at the sun setting in the west. "Looks like we need to be heading out. Do you want to come with us to that little town of Johnsonville? Or is that in the wrong direction for you?"

The man looked toward the sun, then back at Molly and Pepper. "I think I'll head out on foot from here on. I'm sure I'll be able to find another ride heading the right direction soon." He reached out to shake Molly's and Pepper's hand. "It's been a pleasure meeting you two. I'll have to tune in sometime and see if I can hear you on that radio. It'd really be something. Oh—" He began, then dug a scrap piece of paper out of his holey jacket and handed it over to Pepper. "You know where I'll be at," he said with a wink, then waved goodbye, turned and headed out.

"What a strange man," Molly noted as she and Pepper got back inside of the car. She lifted the bag of leftovers to move it to the backseat, but stopped when she noticed something sitting on the top of it. Neatly tucked in the top of the back was a clean ten-dollar bill. Molly picked it up and looked at it. "Looks like he left us something." Molly said.

Pepper grinned when he saw it. "Well, he certainly is a generous man."

Molly moved the bag of supplies to the back seat and Pepper pulled the car into first and they took off.

"You know what?" Pepper asked.

"What?" Molly asked, the wind from the open windows whipping her hair around her face.

"I talked to that Brett for awhile. I really think he's an interesting guy. He says that he's looking for young fresh members for his gang in southern New York."

Molly frowned at him.

"Just think about it Molly! Life around here is getting a little too dull again. I could use a little bit of robbin', stealin' and stuff like that. And he really liked how well you handled that gun."

"Stealing is wrong, Pepper."

"Yeah but we wouldn't really be stealing. It's like Robin Hood. Stealing from the rich to give to the poor, now that's a reputation I could live with, huh, Molly," he said, giving her a little shove from the other side of the car and grinning at her. "Don't you just miss that huge shot of adrenaline? The thrill of doing stuff and getting away with it?"

"We've been homeless before, Pepper. I don't want to give this all up just to go back to like it was before, when we had nothing."

Pepper sighed and rested both hands on the wheel, staring out into the road ahead of them. It was quiet in the car for a few silent minutes, the only sound coming from the V6 engine in the Ford. Molly closed her eyes, thinking about their current life. Wasn't it almost everything she and Pepper had dreamed of? Sure, they weren't making it huge, but they were making money and living a comfortable lifestyle in the middle of a nationwide depression. They had each other, and their music, and that was all that they needed.

"You know what, Molly?"

Molly turned away from the window to look into Pepper's dark eyes.

"You're right."

Molly smiled at him, then nodded.

"We have everything we need right here. I have our own little radio show, my own car, my own fancy guitar, ten dollars cash, and *you* Molly. What more could I possibly want?"

Chapter 13

Molly paced up the hall of the apartment building, then back down impatiently. Her breath seemed to be coming in short bursts as she put her hand to her head, trying to calm herself down. She then opened the door to their apartment and barged in, pacing again in the smaller area.

"Whoa, what's up?" Pepper asked, concerned. They had just finished up their recording for the day and dinner afterward when Mr. Petersen had handed Molly her personal pile of mail.

Molly threw the letter at Pepper, then sat down on the couch beside him. Pepper grasped the handwritten letter carefully, examining the addresses on the outside of the envelope before pulling the letter out.

Dear Molly,

I am not even sure if this is the right Molly, but if we turn the radio dial to exactly the right station we come up with an interesting radio show in which there is a teenage girl named Molly who plays fiddle with her friend Pepper. Now I knew that my Molly was one of the best fiddle players there ever was, even when she was very young, so there is a good chance that you are, in fact, my daughter.

I've looked up all the information I could on you and the only thing that I could find is that you are from someplace in the Midwest and that you have no permanent last name.

Pa, the boys, and I are begging you to come home where you belong. I do not know what may have convinced you otherwise, but you are our daughter whom we love very much and would never want to hurt you in any way.

Pepper looked up at Molly with a shocked look on his face.

She shook her head. "Keep reading," she ordered.

Though it sounds as if you have probably found a better life now, we would still love to see your shining face once again. If I hear nothing back from you before then, I plan to make a trip to New York shortly after Christmastime. Please send me a note and inform me if you are, in fact, my beloved daughter and enlighten me to exactly where you are at.

Your Mother,
Catherine Endersby

Both of them were speechless. They sat silently together on the couch until Pepper put an arm around Molly. "Molly Endersby Thompson. That'll be an interesting name."

Molly stood up suddenly. "Do you know what this means?"

Pepper didn't say anything but looked up to Molly questioningly.

"They know where I am!" She almost shouted.

Pepper just shook his head and stared at her. "So is that really such a bad thing?"

Molly sighed, then shook her head and sat down next to Pepper. "You don't know what kind of life I lived back there! I don't think that I can handle going back to them, or anybody in that hick-town. I cut myself off from them and essentially everybody back in McPherson County; I never intended to go back. No matter what they say, it just won't be the same! It can never be the same." Tears glistened in the corners of Molly's eyes.

Pepper sat there, speechless, with the letter in his hand. He didn't know what to say to her. Obviously there was something he didn't know about Molly and her family. Not that he could know or understand much, having no close family of his own, but he knew there was something embedded deep in Molly's conscious that hurt her so much now.

A few tears dripped down Molly's nose slowly, silently, and she allowed herself to be held by Pepper's strong arms as they sat together wordlessly.

Molly seemed to be in some sort of shock after receiving the letter, but Christmastime felt as though it were a dream for her.

Quite a few times she sat down and started a letter in reply to her mother, but could not seem to get the words that she needed down on paper. Frustrated, Molly wadded up every letter and threw them angrily into the wastebasket. She could only wait and see what would happen.

Pepper seemed excited for Christmas. It meant delicious Christmas baking, presents, and even a Christmas special on the radio for Molly and Pepper. The two often spent the chilly days playing for homeless shelters and a few orphanages.

Shortly before Christmas as the two walked down the sidewalk Molly noted how handsome Pepper looked in his clean leather jacket, long pants that had no holes in them, and his new red hat and mittens. Thankfully nobody recognized them as they walked down the street, their instruments had been delivered beforehand to the homeless shelter where they would be playing.

A flying snowball caught Pepper in the ear, and he rubbed it and turned, irritated, to see who had thrown it. Molly saw three small kids rush to get behind a parked car, the last one slipping on the hard-packed snow and falling onto his face before he got back up to take cover with his friends. Molly could hardly help laughing, she knew that the kids hadn't exactly intended to hit Pepper with the snowball.

Pepper smiled when he saw one of the kids' eyes nervously peek up from behind the hood of the car. Pepper crouched down and rolled a snowball into his hands, then threw it full force in their direction. The snowball hit the top of the hood of the car, then slid, barely missing the kids.

From the other side of the street the kids were quiet. Exactly when Molly began to walk again, they were ambushed. Apparently the other kids had friends, and she heard a laugh right before seven or eight kids ran out with arms full of snowballs.

Molly ran ahead of Pepper but he grabbed the edge of her coat and pulled her to him. "Fight back!" he ordered with another laugh.

Pepper tossed more snowballs at the kids, who gleefully continued to bombard Molly and Pepper. Molly sighed, then scooped up some snow and tossed it back to the kids. The little snowball fight lasted a good fifteen minutes before an adult finally got hit and began yelling at Molly, Pepper, and the kids.

"Quick, let's get outta here!" Pepper exclaimed, out of breath already as he began to run. The kids quickly retreated to their little snow fort.

When they had gotten away from the rants of the man who had been hit, Pepper stopped and laughed. "That was fun!"

Molly agreed. "But we've got to be at the soup kitchen in fifteen minutes. Hope we'll make it."

"Don't worry about it," Pepper said. "Look, we're here already." Pepper pushed open the door and Molly followed him inside. The smell of hot soup on the stove reached her nostrils and her mouth watered. She heard the sound of many voices blending together and the clank of dishes, and turned to look at the people seated at the long tables. So many of them had such sad faces; Christmas was supposed to be a happy time but it was hard for them to be happy when they didn't even have enough money to feed their families.

Molly followed Pepper back into the kitchen where they found a woman named Laura who was in charge of their performance.

"Oh, good, you're here!" she greeted them. "Come out over here to the corner where we've got our little 'stage' set up."

The woman led them over to the corner where they had their instruments. She fiddled with a small microphone until she got it to function properly, then announced, "Thank you folks for coming over to enjoy dinner with us!" She paused for a moment and looked over the faces of all the people who were seated around her, then started again, "we have some special people here to perform for us today. Out of the goodness of their hearts, Molly and Pepper Thompson have agreed to put on a little Christmas performance for ya'll! If you aren't familiar with who they are, if you tune in Thursday nights to CXD you should be able to hear their show. Now I'll get out of the way and let them get their act started!"

There was a brief amount of applause before Molly and Pepper stood up and began with a song. Molly pulled the song out over her fiddle with her bow.

Jingle bells, Jingle bells, Jingle all the way!
Oh what fun it is to ride in a one-horse open sleigh!

Molly heard Pepper's low voice ringing out the familiar tune, and smiled to herself. She loved the sound of men's voices when they weren't afraid to sing.

Pepper stopped for a moment and allowed Molly to add a bit of a fiddle solo. Molly smiled her brightest, attempting to cheer the sober crowd. She saw the edges of some people's mouths begin to curl in the beginnings of a smile.

She opened her mouth and began to sing out the verse as Pepper continued in the chords.

Dashing through the snow, in a one horse open sleigh,
O'er the fields we go, Laughing all the way,
Bells on bobtails ring, making spirits bright,
What fun it is to ride and sing a sleighing song tonight!

Vigorously she sawed away at her fiddle and swirled her colorful woolen skirt as she made her way down the aisle between the long tables. Molly stopped at an especially surly looking man and spiced up her part of the song with a little hokum bowing. Still he didn't smile as she performed especially for him.

A day or two ago,
I thought I'd take a ride,
And soon Miss Fannie Bright
Was seated by my side!
The horse was lean and lank,
Misfortune seemed his lot,
He got into a drifted bank
And we, we got upsot!

With that, she playfully paused her part of the song and tweaked the man's nose, and he pulled back with a start, resulting in laughs from the crowd. Molly smiled brightly and turned away, but not before she noticed the little bit of a grin on his face. Soon the crowd was cheering and clapping along to the tune, loudly singing the refrain.

Before she knew it, the song was over, and Molly and Pepper told some jokes and played a few of their old time songs and a few more Christmas carols before their act was finished. Molly and Pepper each took a bow, then retreated to kitchen to put their instruments away and grab a bowl to join the people in their meal and to listen to the message.

Molly was served her food first and moved to an open spot in the tables next to a middle-aged woman and waited for Pepper. The woman seemed to stare at Molly as she ate her entire meal, Molly noticed and was slightly annoyed. Pepper came and sat down next to Molly and she noticed the woman almost open her mouth as if to start a conversation, but then closed as a preacher-man moved to the front and opened in a sermon, telling the people about the Christmas message.

Molly listened politely as she spooned the warm soup into her mouth. She pulled her warm white sweater closer around herself, grateful for the warm building that she was in. She couldn't imagine what it would be like to be out on the streets at this time.

The message was short and the pastor concluded with an offer of a Christmas basket of food to those who would need it. Shortly after he went back into the kitchen, the woman beside Molly caught her eye and finally found the courage to speak to her.

"I really enjoyed your music," she said simply.

Molly nodded. "Thank you."

There was a bit of an awkward silence as they both tried to think of something to say. Pepper had just gone back into the kitchen and the table was slowly beginning to clear as people begrudgingly made their way back to their everyday lives.

The woman was middle-aged, but her hair was streaked with gray. She had kind brown eyes that seemed to draw Molly to her gaze. Molly opened her mouth just as the woman began to speak, but closed it suddenly as she began to talk. "So, I've heard that you two were both actually drifters? I think I've heard it said that you actually ran away from home a couple years back."

Molly's face turned red as she embarrassedly tried to think of something to say. She had no idea that people knew about her past life; Mr. Petersen had tried hard to keep most of the details a secret.

"Let me tell you something. My daughter ran away a year back. She was a little younger than you, and looked a lot like you, too." The woman reached a bony arm out to grasp Molly's and Molly felt no impulse to pull away as she gazed into the woman's kind eyes. "Abigail felt as if she was just a burden to the family." Her voice began to crack.

"But she wasn't. She was more help than she knew. She had kind of an adventurous spirit like you obviously do. But I can't believe that she would do that. I have no idea where she is now. I've never heard from her. She could be dead." Tears squeezed out of the sides of her eyes, and Molly's lower lip began to tremble as she fought back the tears she could feel as well. The woman's story was already beginning to hit home, and a flood of memories came to her as she listened to the woman speak.

"I can't believe she would do that," the woman kept repeating over and over. "I don't know if it was my fault, but if there was anything I could have done to keep her at home I would have done it. A million times over."

The little girl that was beside the woman tugged on her shirt out of boredom. "Just a minute, Joyce," she said kindly, and continued on. "You don't know what it is like for a mother to lose her child. You'll never know what it is like until you've experienced it yourself. You'll never know. A child may abandon their parents but there's some kind of unbreakable bond that will not let a parent abandon their childen.

"There's nothing you can do about it now, I guess, but I think your ma and pa are probably worried sick about you too. Don't let other kids run away, if you can prevent it. It is so glamorized, but there is really no good reason to leave your home; your family. It cuts families apart, right at the center."

She sighed deeply and heavily, as if the regret was too much for her to bear. She turned and looked into the impatient eyes of her daughter. "Alright, sweetie, I guess it is time to go." She grabbed the girls hand and started across the room toward the main doors, but she stopped before she got too far away from Molly, looking right into her eyes.

"Thanks again, Molly. And please, consider what I've said."

Molly felt the draft of cold air run across the floor, close to her feet, as the woman entered into the freezing temperatures outside. Molly sat still, her legs crossed, on the chair in front of the long table in the dining hall, seemingly unable to move. A flood of memories was making its way through her mind, bothering her conscience beyond her own belief.

Molly didn't even notice when Pepper moved up beside her in the noisy dining hall. She hadn't even acknowledged his presence until she felt his hand on his shoulder.

"Guess what, Molly?" Pepper asked.

Molly looked up to him, her eyes staring into the space behind him, her mind wandering further and further away so that she barely noticed when he answered his question.

"We're going to Boston!"

Molly could hardly believe it. They had only been playing in New York for a few months, but they barely left the city limits. Now Mr. Petersen had a lead he wanted them to pursue in Boston. Excitedly she packed for the day they would leave. A large suitcase was open on her bed.

She held up a denim skirt, then a multicolored one, trying to decide. "Which one, Pepper?" she asked. Pepper trotted over enthusiastically then flopped onto the bed. He grabbed the two from her and inspected them closely and gleefully threw them into the air. "It doesn't matter, Molly. When we get to Boston I'll take you to a huge department store and buy you any kind of skirt that you want."

Molly smiled at his enthusiasm, knowing that his high spirits matched her own, but picked up both of the skirts off the floor and sighed. "Sometimes I wish I could go back to wearing pants again.

They were so much more comfortable sometimes. And they were warmer."

"Aw, who cares, Molly," he said, tilting himself upward to rest his chin on one elbow, "I don't mind when you wear pants. Someday you should just wear them to perform in."

Molly put both of the skirts away and picked out a simple, but pretty calico dress. "Mr. Petersen would have a fit!" she interjected. "Besides, I think he's having someone pick out our wardrobe for when we perform. We have to make a great impression and all that, you know."

Pepper sighed and rolled his eyes. "That darn Mr. Petersen!"

"Well, he does make the most excellent agent." Molly paused her packing for a moment and laid beside Pepper on the bed. He reached for her hand and held it, stroking her fingers carefully and entwining them with his own.

Molly smiled and looked up at him. "Only one more month," she reminded him.

"I can't wait," Pepper replied.

The next day Molly and Pepper boarded the train to their destination. Molly and Pepper conversed together, gleefully infatuated with everything in their private railroad car, from the gleaming glassware and silverware to the comfy chairs to the beautifully-decorated perimeter of the car.

Irritated and slightly embarrassed, Mr. Petersen reminded them that they needed to act professionally at all times.

"But that's the very reason people like us," Pepper argued, "because they can relate to us. Most people are just hicks like us anyway and rather idolize someone who was like them at one point in their lives."

Mr. Petersen just sighed at that and reminded them for the umpteenth time that they needed to at least pretend that they were used to all this stuff.

"This is very important, you two. You can't afford to screw up. We three are going to have a private meeting with a station owner to see if he will play your show on his station, then we are going to be having performances every night for the next two weeks. On the last day we will be having a sort of finale in the enormous building on Fifth Street downtown, with hopefully over eight hundred people attending. So you need to be prepared. Practice your songs. Clean your instruments. Get your sleep. And whatever you do, keep yourself from being distracted."

    Molly felt ready to break under all of the stress she had been put through during the last two weeks. The meeting with the owner of the radio station had gone well, so at least that was off her chest, but she still had their finale to worry about. Molly had tossed and turned almost the entire night before, and so had a long, sleepy day before their evening performance. She was glad that Mr. Petersen had allowed her a short nap. His temper seemed to flare more often lately than it had before, partially because of all the time shortages and commitments he had to keep up. Molly was sure glad that they had him, thus getting irritated even more with Pepper when he decided to mouth off to him. Mr. Petersen had done them good, taking care of all the excruciating details while Molly and Pepper simply performed.
    There was a beautiful dress for Molly to wear that evening along with a suit for Pepper. Anxiously she paced the dressing room in the short half-hour before they would begin. Pepper sat carelessly on a comfy chair, attempting to read a newspaper, but mostly just looking at the pictures.
    "Would you cut that out?" he asked her.
    "What?" Molly stopped and asked him.
    "That pacing around! Geez, you'd think that you'd never performed before. Just settle down. It'll be alright."
    "But what if I mess up? What if they hate me? I know that fiddle music isn't exactly the most in-demand kind of music right now—" she paused. "What if they refuse to listen?" she asked seriously. "I can't stand it when people ignore me. I just can't stand it when good

fiddle music fails to attract attention. It's almost like they're not just refusing my music but rather refusing . ." she stopped for a moment, "me."

Pepper looked up from his newspaper. "Molly, it doesn't always matter what other people think about you. I know that you're not sure about all this, that you think just maybe we should go back to traveling on the road. And generally, sometimes I agree with you." He stood up and walked over to where Molly was standing.

"And it doesn't matter what you think, Molly, I know the majority of the people out there love you." He put his fingers to her chin and softly pulled it up so that she was looking at him. "And don't you ever think for a moment that they're rejecting *you.*" Molly couldn't help but smile at him and Pepper kissed her lightly. "I've got to go now," he said, "I have to talk to Mr. Petersen. But I'll be back in a little bit."

He left, and Molly felt the emptiness of the strange room she found herself in. Quietly, she made her way from the chair back over to a mirror. It was so quiet in the room without Pepper. The silence drove her to biting on her fingernails out of worry and anticipation. She stopped and sat down in front of the lighted mirror. Fingering the items on the dresser in front of her, she thought about what lay ahead. Molly couldn't seem to explain her nervousness.

She looked in the mirror and saw her reflection gazing back at her. *Her* face. The wide green eyes, curved nose and gentle lips. Her dark auburn hair was in a massive heap of beautiful curls around her face, magnificently arranged by a skillful beautician in apprehension of the night before her. She smoothed a hand along her jaw line, thinking about all of the change that she had gone through in the past few months. Her face seemed to glow with all of the powdery makeup she had put on before.

The freckles are gone, she thought suddenly. That was probably why she looked so grown up now. She wiped a little of the white powder off, and unburied a dark freckle underneath. It was just like her, she realized. She could put on a show in front of hundreds of people, all dressed up and professionally playing her part, but underneath she would always be the same. Just a teenage farm girl from humble roots who didn't quite know where she belonged in the world.

She sighed, unbelieving of how exhausted she was. Resting her head in her arms on the table, she closed her eyes slightly. If only she could just sleep now for a bit . . .

"Miss Molly—you need to be ready to go," a woman opened the door and announced. "You're on stage in ten minutes."

Molly blinked her eyes closed for a minute, then opened them and walked onto the stage with her fiddle at her side. Pepper followed behind with his guitar.

The lights seemed too bright for her to perform. Her knees and her hands shook nervously as she made her way across to center stage, where a mike was set up for her.

She reached the center stage much too soon for her liking. She closed her eyes again and opened her mouth in an attempt to begin to speak. But for some reason, Molly felt as if she couldn't do it. So her eyes flew open and she gave Pepper a quick signal, and hastily tucked her violin under her chin, ripping out into a song she knew by heart, called *Forked Deer.*

Pepper's hand sped along into the chord sequence as Molly stood under the lights, pulling out the cheerful, speedy tune that grabbed people's attention. She forced out a smile but couldn't see the people's expressions as she focused her attention on the fingers of her left hand speeding along her old fiddle's faded black fingerboard. Molly was amazed at how beautifully her grandfather's fiddle sounded in the atmosphere she played it in. Nothing else was heard except for the amazing tone of her fiddle and Pepper's guitar.

Pepper played the chords exactly as they needed to be played, his eyes watching Molly as she put every ounce of effort into her performance. He had been able to tell earlier that she had been nervous, agitated and strung-up even, and he could just barely see it now in the way that her movements were just the slightest bit jerkier than they usually were. But he knew that as time went on she would smooth her movements out as she became more accustomed to her surroundings. He watched the audience below, checking for signals from them to see if they approved of this entertainment.

The people at first seemed glued to their chairs, with their eyes glued to Molly. No one spoke as they watched her play, but intently took in what they were seeing. Maybe it was disbelief in their eyes? Pepper couldn't tell.

Pepper played more vigorously and when Molly sensed the little bit of excitement, like a little electric charge in the air, it zapped her with the energy and excitement she kept hidden away most of the time and she unglued her feet from the floor, dancing around the stage and kicking up her heels. She leaned down to look into the eyes of some of the audience, as if playing just for them.

Finally, the invisible wall was broken and one man began to clap to the beat of the music. Molly grinned even wider and played another verse, continuing on the song longer than she originally planned. Others joined in clapping to the beat, and Molly came closer to the microphone so as to avoid her fiddle being drowned out as more and more people clapped. Some people stood up and stomped their feet even, cheering Molly on.

Finally she ended the song with a final sharp note, and the floor erupted in applause. Molly could do nothing but smile and bow cautiously. She waited a good time until the noise died down, and moved forward to the mike confidently.

"In case you didn't already know," she started, "my name is Molly. Molly *Endersby*" For some reason she emphasized her last name. "But soon to be Mrs. Molly Thompson," she said, gesturing to Pepper behind her. "This here is Pepper, my partner and my fiancé. We both have a radio show that can be heard Thursday nights if you tune in to CXD. But that doesn't matter all that much. What we're here for tonight is to put on a show. To play good old-time music for ya'll. This stuff has been buried out back in America's frontier for much, much too long. So we are bringing it back for all you good folks out here on the east coast. So who wants to hear another one?" The crowd shouted their affirmation, and Molly began another song.

It seemed like such a short time before they had to conclude. Mr. Petersen had told them an hour, and no longer. Molly and Pepper strolled off the stage with high spirits. They had barely made it to the back room when Mr. Petersen slammed into them, followed by several other people that Molly and Pepper had seen before, but didn't know.

"I can't believe you," he let out, "I know you guys are impromptu but that—that—"

Molly was ready for the worst, but didn't care. She swallowed a huge gulp of air. It didn't matter. Technically Pepper could fire Mr. Petersen anyway, as he was working for them.

"That was amazing!" Mr. Petersen exclaimed.

Molly exhaled in relief.

"People *will* remember you. And that's what we want."

Molly and Pepper thanked Mr. Petersen and some of the people who were there with him that had helped make the event possible, then turned gratefully toward the dressing room to get changed into comfortable clothes and to get back to where they could get some rest.

"Wait a minute, Molly," Mr. Petersen called out before she had the chance to leave. Molly stopped and turned.

"There's someone waiting for you at the end of the corridor. I haven't ever seen her before. Says she's a Mrs. Endersby."

Chapter 14

Molly felt choked up for a second after Mr. Petersen had told her who was waiting for her. The room seemed to tilt a little bit as her breathing stopped. He couldn't be saying that. He couldn't be saying that her mother was waiting to talk to her. Nervously she began to chew at her fingernails again.

"Molly?" he asked, trying to gain her attention again, "I could tell her to leave if you don't want to talk to her right now."

"No," Molly refused, "I need to talk to her actually. Tell her to meet me in my room in fifteen minutes. Have someone escort her if she doesn't know the way."

Fifteen minutes later, Molly nervously sat in her room. Her eyes darted across the sparsely furnished room. From the uncomfortable bed she was sitting on, to the chair not far away, and back to the clock again. Her fingers tapped anxiously on the wall.

She jumped when she heard the door open. Instinctively she flattened her back against the wall, as if she could get away from what was confronting her right now.

The woman who had entered wasn't very tall, with fading dark hair that was pulled up into a bun over her head. Molly noticed that her pale eyes looked tired when she had found enough courage to look into them for more than just a few seconds. She wore a patterned light blue dress, probably the best one that she had.

Yes, Molly knew that the person who was now sitting across from her was her mother. Tons of thoughts raced through her mind. She had seen this day before in her mind. Molly always thought that she would do something else other that what she was doing right now. She would give her the cold shoulder. She would refuse to see her. Molly would run away. She would metaphorically spit in her parent's face over and over again, even if she hadn't intended it, just like the day she had gotten up and ran away from home.

"Hello Molly," she said, breaking the silence for the first time in ten solid minutes.

"Hi. . . ma." The words were hard to get out for her. "How did you find me?"

Her mother let out a little bit of a soft laugh. "It wasn't hard," she said. "You're getting quite a reputation, even back in the Midwest where you ran from. And from what I've seen tonight, I can see why."

"Molly—" she started again, and reached to touch the strand of hair hanging in front of Molly's face. Molly instinctively jerked away, but then reconsidered what she was going to say when she saw the hurt look in her mother's eyes. But she found it hard to say anything.

"I kind of forgot," Molly's mother said, "I guess you aren't really mine anymore. Your Pa and I—"

"That's right," Molly interrupted. "But just what do you think you're going to make me do? You can't make me go back to that farm. I hate it there. Nobody appreciates me or what I do. Nobody cares. Not even you or pa."

"Molly, your pa and I realize that. We've changed now."

Little tears glistened in the corner of Molly's eyes. "Everyone in that town disliked me."

"No they didn't," her mother told her. "They may have not understood you or maybe even gotten along with you very well, but I guarantee that they didn't hate you."

"Where is Pa and the boys?" Molly asked, changing the subject.

"They're at home still. Or what we call home now. Our family lives in town now. We could only afford a train ticket for one person and your Pa said that I should go."

The look in Molly's eyes begged a question.

"We lost the farm, honey. The bank foreclosed on it not long after you left."

Molly didn't say anything but shook her head. She couldn't believe it. How could they lose the farm that her great-grandfather had worked so hard to establish, and that her father had stubbornly worked to keep? She let her head fall into her hands, and sighed deeply.

"You said that you've changed. How do I know that's true?"

Molly's mother's eyes softened. "We saw our wrong. We used to tell you that we raised you right and that you just were wrong, but now we've realized that we were the ones who were wrong. We can never do anything about all the other people in our little town, but we speak for ourselves now. So we're giving you a choice. We want to have a relationship with our daughter, even though you're almost a completely different person now. If we had our way we'd have you come back to Nebraska and live with us again. But I see that's not possible now, especially with that rogue of a fiancé you have." She smiled, and Molly knew that she was just kidding with her. But Molly thought that her mother was not one to kid.

"But you can come back to us," she continued. "We won't push you to do anything, we won't try to run your life for you. You can live with your new husband wherever you want. But come visit us. Let us back into your life. Let us enjoy you and your family. Or you can ignore us completely like you have been. But it's your choice. We won't intrude on anything you decide."

Molly stood up from where she sat on the bed and made her way to her mother. It was quiet for a minute again as they both stood, contemplating. Finally, Catherine Endersby looked directly into her daughters eyes. She opened her mouth to speak. "You've changed so much," she said quietly, her voice raspy as she choked on the sob that she held down.

Molly slowly, carefully extended her hand and carefully took her mother's hands into her own. "But so have you, ma. So have you."

Molly had never been one to drink. But as she sat in their room that night with Pepper, she sat quietly against the wall with a bottle in her hand, contemplating. Pepper didn't say anything to her, knowing that she just needed some time to be by herself with her thoughts.

She knew that it wasn't completely her family's fault for the predicament that she found herself in now. It was even likely that it was mostly her fault, and that her own character extended the problem even further. How she despised even thinking about going back to that old, nearly deserted dusty old town that she had previously called home. She didn't know why her father would have continued to hold on to a property like that when everyone else was leaving or getting foreclosed on.

But Molly had thought that she would never have to see her family again. She thought that if she never sought out her parents, they would never seek out her. She still couldn't believe what had just occurred. She thought she had left everything behind . . .she wanted nothing to do with her old life. Molly thought that she had run away from her past.

"That's it!" she said aloud, and Pepper turned to look at her. Her cheeks turned rosy red as she realized that she had spoken something aloud that probably made no sense to Pepper. But she just shook her head, looking away from him.

Molly thought some more. But that's exactly what it boiled down to. She decided to speak to Pepper again, talking slowly. "You can't run away from your past."

Pepper looked at her again, understanding in his eyes now. He knew it wasn't his battle but he wanted to help Molly in any way that he could.

"You can sure try," he said, "but in the end it won't get you anywhere. Sometime you have to turn and face it head on."

She was quiet and turned away again, her eyes bloodshot from the incredible amount of stress that had been put on her the last few days and from the tears that had been shed less than an hour ago. Molly leaned her head against the wall, further fluffing her ruined, fuzzy hair.

"You're right," she said, almost in a whisper. "It doesn't matter what I do, as long as I quit running away from this mess I've put myself into. I can't run away any more."

Molly and Pepper rode the train together the next week. Molly felt a sense of foreboding as she listened to the train's clickity-clack, clickity-clack, pulling her closer and closer to her old home. As she looked out the window of the train, watching the scenery fly by, she almost laughed to herself. It had taken Molly and Pepper months and months of traveling to get here, but it would only take them a couple of days on the train to get back.

Pepper gripped her hand tightly, reassuringly. She smiled up at him, and she felt a warm tingle go down her spine when he grinned back. He looked so handsome in the clothes he wore now. A clean shirt, shoes, and pants that actually reached past his ankles. His rust-colored hair was combed flat on his head, and his face was scrubbed clean, holding no trace of dirt, and bringing out his shining brown eyes. Molly was sure that he would make a wonderful husband, and eventually, father. But there was a part of her that missed his boyish tousled hair, his bare feet and slight bit of dirt around his face.

"Whatcha' thinking about?" He asked.

"I don't know," she lied, but then changed her mind. "Home. Pa. The boys."

He nodded in agreement.

"But I'm also thinking about what we're going to do when we get back to New York. I wonder how long they're going to keep our show on the radio."

Pepper gently ran a finger down the side of her face. "You want to be out on the road again," he said softly, and she looked up at him. "I can see it in your eyes."

Molly pulled her violin closer to her feet in the rumbling train car. "I guess I do. I can't remember the last time we actually had to play for a meal." He smiled at her. "Well, yes, actually I do remember. But it was such a long time ago. There's just a part of me that wants to roam, be out on the road, to work hard for a living. I can't stand being in one place too long."

"I agree. I'm so glad you're like that Molly, 'cause I am too. Whatda say that as soon as we get back to New York, we resign and head out again, and this time we'll go all the way. From one end to the other. All the way from good old New York to Californiee."

Her eyes lit up for a second, but suddenly dimmed again. "But what about Mr. Petersen? And about all we "owe" to the people who listen to us? We can't just get up and leave."

"Sure we can," he replied. "That's what reruns are for. We've got quite a stash of cash stacked up now. We don't need to worry about money, or the people who listen to us on the radio, or Mr. Petersen."

"Well, let's at least finish up the season. And let's wait until it's a little warmer."

Molly's mother was in the row next to them on the other side. Molly couldn't believe that Mr. Petersen had allowed them to go back to Nebraska without too much of a fight. But then again, Pepper had a way with convincing people.

She and Pepper were going back to meet her father and brothers, and perhaps would stay for a week or so, though she knew her mother wanted her to stay longer.

"We've got to switch trains here," Pepper announced as soon as he felt the train slowing down the slightest bit. When the train had come to a stop, Molly, Pepper and her mother stepped off onto the platform. It had turned out that their next train was late, so they had a good hour or so to burn before their train would be there.

Molly paced back and forth with her fiddle case in her hand. Pepper and her mother sat on a bench, obviously more patient than she was. Other people strolled around, being careful not to get too far from the station. The warm sun of March was finally beginning to penetrate the snow that was now in small patches on the ground. They were almost to Nebraska and the climate was considerably warmer than what they were used to in New York.

Molly stopped pacing for a moment to look around herself. She saw signs of the depression all around her. People's suitcases were small, but some of them were large as they held all that they had, to start a new life on another side of the country. The businesses by town that she could see from the station weren't doing too well either. Many of them were closed with "out of business" signs hanging in the windows. She was frustrated at the problems that the people of her nation faced. It wasn't like it was their fault that the economy was terrible.

Suddenly her eyes moved to a bush growing near the station. There were whitish-pink blossoms sprouting out from it in the warm spring air, oblivious to the dark colors of the depression going on all around them. She smiled, appreciating the beauty of the bush before she realized what the beautiful little flowers were. *Blackberry blossoms!*

The sight invigorated her, and she set down her fiddle case, pulling out her fiddle, then her bow. Her eyes conveyed a message to Pepper, who took out his guitar and put it onto his lap, ready for Molly to begin. She sighed softly, then let out the sweet beginning notes. It was too bad that the song didn't have any words to it. Or as far as she knew, there were no words to it. Maybe there were words to it, it was just that the song itself was so old that they had been lost with time . . .

As she played, she didn't care if anyone stopped to listen. She didn't care if people ignored her as they walked by. She didn't even care if they liked it or not. Her arm pulled out the notes of the song automatically and though she was playing the song with her arms; pulling out the tune with each bow stroke, it wasn't exactly what she was thinking about at the time. She was thinking about when she had first run away from home, and had been hungry, cold and tired every night. Then she had met Pepper, her now fiancé, and thought about what he had been like when she first met him. Pepper had filled a big, lonely hole that had been in her life, and now—she was hoping—having her family together and supporting of her would finish filling that little bit of a hole that was left.

Her life was like fiddle music, she realized. There was a time for a single fiddle to play, to be heard all by itself. But if heard too often it would get lonely. It needed guitar backup, a person to back you up, to support you and complete you. A fiddle and a guitar fit together perfectly and complemented each other in every way. But the more instruments, or family, that was added, made the song even more complete. There was nothing like playing fiddle music with a lot of other instruments, making it sound amazing. And it didn't even matter if it was a depression, if the banks were failing, people losing their jobs left and right. Like a fiddle song that slowed down for a verse, it sped up again for the chorus. And so she was inspired that the nation's depression woes would not last forever.

Before she knew it, the song was over, and the small crowd that had gathered burst into applause. Molly started, not even noticing that they had gathered. Her mother cheered loudly for her as well, and Molly thought she saw a tear forming near the brim of her eye.

In the heat of the moment, she held her grandfather's fiddle triumphantly in the air with one hand, her bow in the other. It was a symbol to her now. Not just her means of making a living, but a reminder of everything that had happened to her in her life in the past year. She didn't even feel ridiculous holding it out like that, and neither did the small crowd around her, who cheered louder.

The train pulled up to the station only a few seconds later, and Molly quickly packed up her violin, ready for whatever was to come.

The next day they arrived in the small town that was close to the farm where Molly had lived for most of her life. Molly's hands shook nervously in her lap in the minutes before they got to the little station. There were only two other people who had gotten off at the same place.

The sun seemed warmer here, melting any small patches of snow that was left and warming her body. Molly had to blink hard as she came out into the sun. She stepped out of the train, looking around the familiar one-horse town with anticipation. It seemed like it had been so long since the last time she had been there.

Pepper grasped her hand reassuringly. Together they walked to the house that Molly's family now called home near the outskirts of town. Molly walked nervously, her fingers playing with her hair then moving down to smooth her dress. When her mother pointed out the house, Molly almost stopped in her tracks and turned to run away. But she knew that she couldn't run away any more, so she bravely walked forward.

What would her father and her brothers do? Give her a lecture? Remain distant and disapproving? Her head swirled with the thoughts rushing through her mind.

Her father opened the door and stood on the porch, staring out at them as they came up the walk. He looked the same way that Molly remembered him, except for with maybe a little more gray hair. Her walk slowed as she saw him come off the porch. What was he going to do? Surely he wouldn't strike her . . .

She braced herself as he hurried toward her. Her father paused for a moment in front of her, then swept her into his arms in a huge hug. It was unexpected for her, and for a moment she just stood there, standing tall. Her mother came up behind and hugged her as well. She couldn't believe when her brothers joined in the group hug. She didn't know what it was, but Molly felt something break in her, and she hugged them back. A flood of emotions flooded her as she stood there. Why had she run away in the first place? It seemed like she couldn't remember as she stood in her family's arms. But it felt like she truly belonged there.

Chapter 15

Molly wiped her hands on a towel, glad that she was finally finished with the dishes from that afternoon's meal.

"Mommy? Can I go outside with daddy and help him work on the tractor?"

She looked down at the little boy who was her son and smiled. "Sure you may. Just make sure he doesn't let you sit on his lap and drive it until he's knows it's fixed for sure."

The two year-old ran outside to find Pepper, or Daniel, as Molly had begun to call him. Molly looked out of the dusty window of the little house and sighed. So much had happened in the last eleven years.

Molly and Pepper didn't have their show anymore, though reruns could occasionally be heard if someone was to tune in to just the right station. Molly and Pepper had been married in New York shortly after they returned from their visit to Molly's parents. They had stayed with Mr. Petersen in New York doing shows for another year. After that, Molly and Pepper had followed the longing of their hearts and went out on the road again, having no permanent home for themselves; riding the rails, sleeping under the stars almost every night, and playing for their meals.

It took them a couple years, but they had made it all the way from New York to California again, and had spent a few months working in the orchards before they got bored of that and started back east again. The only problem or care they seemed to have was "all that good money just sitting". Molly and Pepper were used to living on such a little amount that they weren't sure what to do with all the excess. They had found an answer though when they went back to see Molly's parents.

Pepper had grinned hugely that day as he signed a check to the bank that had foreclosed on Molly's family farm. It wasn't like a lot of other people had money for a farm, and so he had gotten it for a very good price. Molly's family moved back in the next week and as far as Molly's choice of a spouse—her parents had no doubt that he would be a wonderful man for her. Pepper and her father had gotten along from the start.

Their travels had somewhat ceased after the time Molly told Pepper that she was pregnant with their first child. They had moved to Nebraska to work on the family farm, but still had plenty of time for traveling, though now more often they did it in their Model A. Their daughter, Emma, had been born in the spring nine years ago. She was the pride of her parents, with spunky red hair and a lanky frame just like her father. That is, until their son Matthew was born, and Emma had to share the spotlight. He was a little more like his mother, not just in character but also with brown hair and freckles.

Molly smiled as she made her way outside to the porch. She was so glad that Pepper could handle at least a partially normal life, without all of the traveling. Molly loved traveling, but there was also a part of her that liked to be in one place, as if she were rooted there and truly belonged.

She was glad too, that after so many years, the depression was starting to lose its grip on America. Finally job stability was coming back, and businesses were able to open again. But what made her even more happy was that the dust finally had died down a little. Pepper and her father were working on a new theory with farming, a thing where they rotated and regularly rested the land so that it would never turn to dust again.

Molly hung onto the railing of the porch, looking out to see if she could spot Pepper and Matthew or Emma. Emma came running towards Molly as soon as she saw her. "Ma?" she asked when she came up to the porch with her. "When are we going to go on a road trip again? After the baby's born?"

Molly smiled and put a hand on her slightly swelling tummy, ready for baby number three to be here already. "We'll see," she answered. "Whenever your pa wants to go."

"Well I hope it's soon," Emma said, "but I've got to practice my fiddle some more. And with that, she went inside to get the half-sized violin that Pepper had bought her.

Shortly after Pepper came out of the barn and walked to the porch where Molly stood. He stopped before he got too close to her.

"How's it going, Molly?" he asked gently. She looked down the porch steps into her husband's eyes.

"I've still got to decide what we're going to have for dinner tonight when Ma and Pa come over. But other than that it's going great." Molly reached for his hands, but Pepper snatched them quickly then pulled her around so that he was sitting on the porch with Molly in his lap. He kissed her tenderly, and when he pulled away Molly smiled, noticing Matthew toddling toward the porch steps where they sat. She picked him up and held him close, treasuring her child that she held in her hands.

Molly was so grateful for everything that she had. She had a beautiful home, a family and a wonderful husband who loved her. She couldn't ask for anything more. Because Molly now knew exactly where she belonged, and she wouldn't trade it for the world. Molly often thought of those few months she had spent alone on the road. She knew that she wouldn't ever have to go to bed again alone, wondering where she was going to go and how she was going to get fed the next day. She treasured the adventure she had over the years with Pepper, and with their soon to be three children, it only served to make the adventure even more exciting.

She heard fiddle music sailing over the air toward where they were sitting. Though Emma was only nine years old, Molly had already taught her tons of songs on her little fiddle. Molly squeezed Pepper's hand, grateful once again for everything she had. She heard Emma switch from a hoedown to a slower waltz, then once again to a faster, but very familiar song.

Molly stood to go inside to get her grandfather's old fiddle, and Pepper followed her, sensing what she was going to get. He found his guitar and brought it outside, and Molly came after, holding her fiddle in her hands. Molly and Pepper walked over to where Emma was in the grassy field near their house, followed by the toddling Matthew. The sun shone brightly down on them, the huge blue expanse of the sky stretching out for miles above them, the wind only teasing at their hair. Molly smiled as she brought her fiddle to her chin and Pepper strummed his guitar. Together they played with their daughter like they had so many times before, pulling out the high sweet notes of the song *Blackberry Blossom*.

About the Author

Mattie Richardson wrote her first book, *Appaloosy* when she was thirteen years old and published it when she was sixteen. Since then she's published two other children's books, *Dusty's Trail* and *Golden Sunrise*. In December of 2011 she graduated high school early and began her first semester of college in January. Though now she has less time to work on her writing, she still enjoys writing her historical fiction horse stories and other novels. When she's not working on her studies or writing, she enjoys riding horse, playing fiddle, guitar and drums, speaking to schools and other groups about her books and writing, as well as typesetting and editing others' books.

ORDER FORM

Use this convenient order form to order more books by Mattie Richardson

PLEASE PRINT:

NAME: _____

ADRESS: _____

CITY: _____

STATE: _____ ZIP: _____

PHONE: _____

_____ Copy (ies) of Blackberry Blossom @ 9.95 each=_____

_____ Copy(ies) of Appaloosy @ 7.95 each=   _____

_____ Copy(ies) of Dusty's Trail @ 7.95 each=   _____

_____ Copy(ies) of Golden Sunrise @ 7.95 each=   _____

Postage: $2.55 for the first book, $1.00 for each additional:
                                                 _____

Total amount enclosed: _____

Send order form and check or money order to:

Mattie Richardson/Appaloosy Books
5749 139th Ave. SE
Sheldon, ND 58068

Thank You!

Other Books By Mattie Richardson

Children's historical fiction books:

Appaloosy

Storm is a beautiful brown Appaloosa stallion belonging to the famous Nez Perce tribe. He hates living the domesticated life and is determined to escape and run free across the open west.

Instead, he is given to a young brave named White Feather, and surprisingly, the two bond together as everlasting friends. But when war breaks out in the Idaho wilderness Storm's life is turned upside-down.

After being sold twice and facing many unique challenges, he comes to live with Faith, a young girl living on a small farm with her family. The two soon become inseparable, and Storm is content to live with her for the rest of his days. But when he is stolen by rustlers heading west, once again circumstances have spun his life around.

When he is finally able to free himself, he must decide between returning to Faith…or the chance to be free.

Dusty's Trail

WANTED: YOUNG, SKINNY WIRY FELLOWS NOT OVER 18. MUST BE EXPERT RIDERS WILLING TO RISK LIFE DAILY. ORPHANS PREFERRED. WAGES $25 PER WEEK.

When young Levi Anderson reads this ad in a local newspaper, he can hardly resist the urge to saddle up and head out for a new job.

Trouble is, his horse Dusty doesn't think it's such a good idea.

Dusty enjoys his quiet life working on Levi's small family ranch; taking Levi to town, chasing cows, fixing fence and sometimes even horseracing with the neighbors. He couldn't imagine leaving.

Levi steals away in the middle of the night, taking the reluctant Dusty with him. Dusty may sometimes rear and buck, gallop and balk, but he tries to be good and really is in with his friend and rider Levi for the long run. And the more they gallop on those wild runs with the "Pony Mail," the closer they bond as friends.

But when Indian trouble arises, endangering the Pony Express stations and even Levi's life, with Dusty prove to be a worthy mount?

Golden Sunrise

Cheyenne is a beautiful Golden Palomino mare raised in Northern Texas during the early 1800's.

When her owner, Jared, is convinced to become a volunteer soldier for the emerging Texas fight for independence, she must travel with him along with his friend Rueben into San Antonio, Texas. Jared has orders to help defend the famous Fort Alamo against Mexican forces, and the more Cheyenne learns about Texas' fight for independence; the more the feisty mare is determined to help Jared to fight in any way she can.

Along the way the two fight in battles, hide a cannon near the town of Gonzalez, and meet new friends like James Bowie and Davy Crockett.

But the Mexican forces are set on extinguishing the fire of Texan independence in any way they can… will Jared and Cheyenne make it through the war? And will the Texas flag fly for freedom?

Coming soon

Day and Night

Tucker and Shiloh are two horses that are as different as day and night. Though they are brothers, Tucker is a tall, strong, and dependable bay while Shiloh is a short gray with a temper.

The two were raised together on a farm in northern Missouri, until the unavoidable conflict of the Civil War begins to work its way into Missouri and "Bleeding Kansas," and their owner is forced to sell the two young horses.

Tucker is sold to a family in the north while Shiloh is sold to a Confederate soldier in the south. Will the two horses ever see each other again? Or, more importantly, will they make it through the conflict that ultimately resulted in more than 600,00 American casualties?

The Secret of the Hemlock Forest

Sunshine is just an ordinary girl. Living an ordinary life, going to an ordinary school, facing ordinary obstacles of the ordinary fourteen year-old…like what clothes to wear, how to make friends, or what she should do Saturday night. The only thing that sets her off from the others is that she often spends time alone in the Hemlock forest near her home. People wonder why she spends her time there—there are stories told of people going into the forest and never coming out again, about crazy people and animals who live there, or other strange happenings. There are fables and legends about the creatures that live deep inside the forest. The hemlock forest is rarely visited, by humans anyway.
Maybe there is a real reason why people don't go into the forest. But Sunshine just sits and relaxes within the realms of the dark forest, thinking about the creatures that were said to live there,

and contemplating just how ordinary and unsocial she really is. But when she hears a strange sobbing in the woods one evening she couldn't help but follow the sound. What she stumbles across is something unusual; something that may even teach her a lesson about her own life…something extraordinary.